Ana and her m birds

ISABEL RAMÓN DE LA IGLESIA

DEDICATION

To all the women in the world, whose stories were never told.

CONTENTS

1 A PECULIAR RAIN

I always thought the past was a road never to be trodden again.

That morning, when dawn broke and the stirring of changing temperatures formed a thin cloud, the unexpected happened. It rained scorpions. Not cats and dogs, neither the proverbial frogs, but small yellow Mediterranean scorpions, that in their dozens amidst the droplets, poured down onto the far end of the garden or 'the back' as I lately thought of it because the title of garden seemed an overstatement when observing the state of it.

The breeze that had precipitated that bizarre downpour grew louder and louder voicing my thoughts against the arid ground, or it might have been the reverberating patter of the malign creatures crashing their shells against the soil and certain stones.

It was one April day in England, on the south coast, 1990.

Ana and her messenger birds

"There are women …"

The breeze echoed around and through me: "there are women like flags, for whom men will die or fight to their very last breath. Carnal banners undulating destinies woven through infinite nights of passion…"

I covered my ears and closed my eyes once, twice… but the breeze continued relentlessly: "there are also diamond shaped women of unyielding matter, whose souls it is said to be anchored to the bedrock of the deepest sea, waiting for the eventual storm that might submerge the human spirit. There are women forged in the warmest of hearths, between aromatic recipes and baking practices, those who adopt marzipan shapes where mankind holds its pace (at their tables), to take interminable bites at their never-ending labour…There are saint-women, little madams, and women martyrs, bitches and witches, sirens and muses, wallflowers, fragrant roses, discarded weeds…there are women as there are flowers" whispered that April breeze its old song. Its murmuring force travelled through the four corners of my domesticity, creating whirlwinds here and there, lifting upwards the scarce goodness of my once fertile garden, taking it out to the high seas which that morning appeared calm and docile some twenty yards below the left fence of 'the back'.

It was obvious to all that the fences erected around the house to prevent or minimise marine erosion could not cope with the inclemency of that bizarre April weather lashing that stretch of beach and my garden from nowhere, as the rain seemed to gravitate over our house. Beyond the garden fence and the immediate beach there were no signs of rain, no breeze, no scorpions, and no one seemed surprised, neither people nor their dogs, who roamed up and down the coastal paths oblivious of their owners.

My home was perched on a promontory, half indented in the hillside that formed the peninsula, where the fishing village of Scarton had not dared to expand. The lane that reached it descended perpendicular to the waterline, while the promontory and the tail end of the lane were sheltered from the northern winds by the higher ground of the village. The house was artificially levelled but the garden had been allowed to follow the gentle gradient of the hillside where the afternoon met the evening, and a chimerical back-gate leading to the public beach marked the lowest south-western spot. That unusual position of the entire property created a benign microclimate generally milder during any season than that of the rest of the far-off neighbouring houses.

On sunny mellow days the unbroken reflection of the ocean kisses the white walls of the cottage with Mediterranean brightness without equal and on bad weather-days, the stormy thrusts only mistreat the western fence on their way inland, following the topography of the hillside under which the house shelters. With fair or unfair weather, in winter or summer, my home was an oasis to all those who inhabited it…well…that was the case until that rare atmospheric phenomena began, with those unusual breezes and the unnatural drought in my garden. These were strange weather days even to English standards and I was at a loss because I could not talk about them with the rest of the villagers to ascertain its source and duration. I was a welcome stranger amongst a small community of seafarers, and I did not want to change my status in it, for some breeze or another.

The breeze that morning loitered with some purpose at ground level where the rained scorpions had been buried under the displaced dust. Once it settled nothing remained for the eye to see but innocuous sterility. After the temperature also settled for the day, the wind died down and calm prevailed about me.

As always, I certainly cut a melancholy picture, on a chair in the middle of the patio, like every other morning that April. My hands lay on my lap forgotten as my aunt used to do when deep in thought. Such fruitless hands they seemed to be, such empty limbs and inscrutable palms; only that wedding-ring with no reason to be on that finger any more…A blackbird was startled without an obvious reason and fled from his post on the fence. I also interrupted my watch and went back indoors, straightened my clothes and my mind, and began the ritual of our daily living. I poured tea into two cups, buttered two cold toasts, composed the breakfast tray, and took it upstairs with the economy of movement developed after monotonous repetition.

The curtains in our bedroom were still drawn together, though a slim sunbeam had penetrated the darkness and rested on his cheek, disturbing his sleep. Ed heaved under the pressure of unconscious pain, gripping the rim of the bedclothes with his right hand like a blind claw. His brow was contracted. "Today we have tea and toast for a change" was my morning-call as usual. Loud, to bring him back from his purgatory and he in turn opened his eyes to follow my nursing exercises of curtain-opening, pillow-puffing, mild smiles, and mindless chatter with quiet indifference. But I had begun to understand his moods by now and though I knew what living in constant agony and dread was, I would never tell him that I knew how he felt. I would never demean his hell because unlike his, my days were not counted; though purposeless and barren my days were many still to come but he was dying, fighting his last battle. I knew how he felt…because something in me was dying, around me dying.

While he consumed his unnecessary breakfast, more as a habit than the vital pleasure of healthy beings, I observed the Atlantic waters through the window and the fallen scorpions sprang to my memory.

"Ed, did you know it rained this morning and the back looks drier than a vineyard in August?"

"Did you get wet?"

"No, but …are yellow scorpions deadly?"

"I shouldn't think so, why?"

"Just curiosity", and with that answer we reached one of those gaps of quiet reflection, lost in our own observation of the ocean outside. The horizon line straight and certain, made all kinds of embarkations disappear to who knows what remote destinations.

"Doctor Miller rang earlier while you slept."

"Is the morphine ready to be collected?"

"He will be delivering it, but he still seemed uncertain about my nursing aptitude. He went over the instructions again and offered me professional counselling. Perhaps he thinks me a bit too emotional to cope with death."

"And are you?" Ed asked, half waiting for a confession and half dreading it.

"When the time comes…my actions will be my answer."

"You never answered my three years' worth of questions."

"We should know the person by their actions."

"A silent past mutilates the prospect of a future."

But I did not answer. I was tired of the crossword-game that had invariably led us to an impasse during our marriage. We never fought openly. We always made our way through disagreements in a crabbish way, without confrontations.

I sat at the foot of the bed; my attention still fixed on the ocean. Inadvertently doing so, as it was my habit when troubled or thinking, I proceeded to feel my hands, to touch the knots of my fingers, to fidget with my only ring, while the morning breeze echoed against the window: "There are women…many kinds of women who walk the earth leaving no mark on it…"

"There are many kinds of women, Ed…"

"As many as there are kinds of men," he echoed finishing his breakfast.

"What type of woman would you say I was if you were to assess me, as a eulogy, you know? The essence of what you think of me." This time our silence glided, interwoven through events, disagreements, and intimacy we never shared when we played marital games, being but two strangers married on a blind date.

"I shall die soon, Ana, taking my memories wherever I

deserve to rest...and yours may fade the quickest in my deterioration into dust because you remain a stranger to me, to this day. I can't possibly know what epitaph to give you, my dearest Ana."

I held his eye without resentment. We were at peace with each other. We had never meant to hurt the other. We had been *that* close to paradise but missed the last turning, and now we were marooned together at the gates of his death and the signs were unmissable.

Two ships cross paths on the high seas; they exchange salutes and pass in opposite directions to unknown destinations. However, that sea was growing lonelier in our last voyage, while I found that my raft was sinking, having lost my compass as well.

A handful of sun rays played with his hair, adding lustre to the silver that crowned his tempered face. The blue of his eyes was soft and warm and giving. His hand beckoned me shyly. His ship was throwing a tentative lifeline and I needed to have my navigation chart read before I sank under the weight of my past.

"There are women like the sirens of the reefs..."

The wind whistled as it passed by the window. I sat by his side and held his hand between mine in my lap. "What would you like to know?" I offered and the seconds passed in suspended animation, as he picked and chose the magical question among others, a million others he had for me.

"Ana, why did you marry me...I mean...what made you want a complete stranger so far from your country?"

"I was in trouble. Toni, my ex...my first husband had been

looking for me since March 84."

"Toni, your ex-husband?" Ed interjected with incredulity.

"My first husband", I repeated by way of apology.

"Did he find you then?" Ed cued me avoiding a thousand natural questions.

"Someone matching his description had been enquiring about me at the British Consulate where I worked. Alicante is a small city, too provincial to hide identities, besides, I knew his pattern of behaviour from experience but that time he was determined enough to lose his anonymity in the process, if that made me come out of mine in panic."

"But why?"

"I am a threat to his political ambition."

"Has he hurt you?" His eyes were darkening with concern.

"He did, in the past", but a cloud watered my eyes before I could control the emotions so long buried. It was that overwhelming silent grief which had kept me in a barren limbo for so many years and would eventually have drained my life but for Ed, Ed and his companionship, Ed who needed me.

But now Ed and his concern had pushed ajar the door to my secret chamber of horrors. I was very vulnerable to his kindness and had always been. I wept unhurriedly, sadness rolling down my face dropping on my lap, dampening my arid thighs, observed by a quiet Ed and a quieter room and a still horizon swallowing ships quietly.

Life had paused for a while to let me hurt as I should, to let the right man ask me another question, but he let the moment pass as it came and I began to move around the room, shunning voluntary confessions and clearing the medicine tray, then I gave him the morning dose. That done, I opened the window to let the fresh air in and old ghosts out, lingering in that captivating view of a ship sailing southwards, out of the Solent in vertical motion, penetrating the edges of sky and sea as she disappeared between the two, drawn by the perfect abyss.

When I turned, Ed was dozing semi-reclined on his pillow, perhaps in a happy slumber after our newfound togetherness and somehow, it did not matter anymore that the past emerged if it gave him a peaceful departure.

Thus, we commenced our question and answer game.

2 THE DIGGING WORKS

As customary since Ed had come back from his self-imposed exile in Spain, we had taken to sitting in the conservatory from lunch until dusk, which enabled me to continue with the freelance translations that were my employ, first in Spain for the British Consulate and later in England for a publisher in London.

We had arranged the furniture to accommodate Ed and his needs around my working area and in the living room, converting the sofa into a daybed with vistas to the beach and in sight of the garden, and we also had installed an electric chair-lift and made room for his wheelchair.

The afternoon of the day that rained scorpions we lounged about in the conservatory, Ed reading a book with an inscrutable cover, while I made vain attempts at translating the third chapter of mine from Spanish to English. I had already read the book to understand the plot, the characters and the author, being now stuck with the task of reading it a second time, to decipher the writing style before the actual translation. I was told I had to produce this literary work in a different language, without compromising the author's readership and the integrity of the story told..."Los pájaros de buen Agüero", (The messenger birds) but the lines seemed to move up and down the page in waves and their ebb and flow made the reading impossible. Their distracting rhythm followed the pattern of a distant murmur outside, at the back. I looked through the French windows and ...I noticed a heavy patter of rain, again. It brought those yellow scorpions to my memory. A glance at the weather, another at Ed and the question floated spontaneously: "Have you ever heard of raining scorpions?"

Ed blinked with amusement. "Cats and dogs yes, frogs and fish too but not scorpions. Is the book causing you problems?"

"No, no, I just wondered."

I found myself doubting some of my senses beside the common. I resumed my reading, a line, another, the same line again. There was no use; those yellow scorpions must still be there (if they have ever been) so, compelled by a sudden urge and curiosity never felt before, I ventured out beyond the comforts of the conservatory against Ed's recommendations, and I stood there stupefied.

The desolation was shocking. A malign blight had overrun the whole garden; and the marvel was that the rain droplets were hammering the ground without wetting it, blowing little puffs of dust. The soil was drier now than in the morning.

I stepped shyly over the once lush lawn that, now a parched savannah's soil, cracked under my feet.   The rain ceased to touch me as I advanced among the several isles of moribund bedding that dotted the "back".

I stretched my palms ahead of me to verify the meteorological wonder. Nothing. All was well except that uncanny breeze filtering through my fingers, caressing and turning my wedding ring, while the dry rain persisted in hammering the arid soil.

A sweet scent of first rains over thirsty lands ascended and lingered like a transparent mist of invisible properties.

I turned my head to the conservatory with euphoria, to call Ed but no sound was uttered. The rain was falling heavier beyond the perimeter of the garden, forming an inscrutable curtain, through which only the blurred contours of the house were discernible.

I reproached myself for my hyperactive imagination. Had I completely lost all sense of reality? Apparently, since the morning.

To no avail I invoked the old order of things. I thought of Ed, a shopping list, my work deadline but all was in vain; the natural laws of nature appear not to have relevance anymore inside the vacuum of my "garden". I wandered further into it, to the left, nearing a black spot which had not been there yesterday, and the closer I got to the shadow, the darker and more solid it grew until its contours became visibly mobile and human.

It was the figure of an old woman, sturdy, of generous size, dressed in an amorphous array of black layers of skirts and shawls or scarves. She had materialised there, where the midday received shelter, at the far end of the southern fence, where the ground rolled gently trying to escape through the opened gate, westwards, to the beach below.

"Hi there!!". I called out to scare the intruder, but the phantom-like creature only jerked her head for an answer. In doing so I recognised a familiar countenance.

I got closer...

"Is it you Anita? "

Oh dear, that voice...a fluid cold penetrated my blood. That face, her dear face, her marzipan shape wrapped in dark layers of chocolate memories....

" Is that you Yaya?" I uttered clumsily, childishly. My knees lost substance and sunk under my weight, kneeling me on the ground from which a murmuring breeze sipped through, rose, and spread:

"There are women forged in anvils"

She must have heard it too because she stopped her digging, and finding a protruding tree stump nearby (never there before), my grandmother crouched and sat on it, folding her various skirts, under-garments and apron around her legs, in a prudish manner. She untied the knot of her black headscarf in her usual fashion, with deliberate slowness and folded it, auguring the intimacy of some secret. I found a mound of moist soil where I sat.

"Do you know I have been meaning to dig this patch for ages, but I could never find the appropriate time and weather?"

I glanced back at the house, but the rain curtain obfuscated the view.

There was still a lingering doubt. A twitch of

self-consciousness was admonished. All in vain. Instead, I felt an overwhelming togetherness, thick with memories shared, memories passed on, inherited.

"What are you doing this far from home Yaya?" I tentatively enquired; as if travelling such long distances at her age was all that ludicrous, notwithstanding the fact that she was dead, twenty years since, buried, and I was conversing with her.

"Just a bit of digging. I can see you have never done it yourself.........but I learnt how to, during the war, you know? I dug many ditches and trenches during that wretched time…come on, pick up that other spade and help me finish this in time, will you?"

I obeyed sheepishly.

What else could I do?

We were half an hour busying ourselves in that aimless job, when she stood up, and glancing sideways, she asked in my ear:" Do you know our family never came from Salamanca but from Guernica, up in the real north?"

I sat on the edge of the growing hole, to invite more of her disclosures. Yaya remained standing but leaning on her spade, inside the hole in a solid form of black clothing.

"Is that why granddad was never found after the war? " I spurred on.

"No, my child, no, it's because I couldn't bring myself to offend his memory."

"Was he a Fascist? "

"Worse."

Worse? What could have been worse than a fascist in that war, I thought.

Ana and her messenger birds

"Franco only allowed some of the dead to be exhumed. My husband was never officially dead. He belonged to the army of unmarked, unknown corpses that were moved around the country for political means. I never claimed his remains. He wouldn't have wanted his daughters to know of his fate, of the shame of his death, nor would he have wanted to provide political ammunition to the regime by the publicity of his execution."

"Was he killed by his own side? Why?"

"It's a long story…but if you have some idling time, I have plenty of it to spare myself."

I looked back at the conservatory, beyond the curtain of rain, wishing for Ed to come out and witness the scene, to give it reality, while at the same time dreading it.

"It happened long ago. Did you hear of the bombing of Guernica, on a Monday afternoon like this, in 1937? " Yaya asked.

"It's well known now but why wasn't I told our family history when I was told so many other stories? "

"Kind of shameful; not only the events that forced us south but the brutality we lived under, during our exodus, when the war finished and years after…many years after". She sighed while wiping her brow and eyes with an oversized white handkerchief brought out of the black folds of her multiple skirts.

Ed began to call me, and his "Ana are you alright?" had permeated the downpour, startling us. I sprang to my feet alarmed by his anxious tone and looked in the direction of his voice.

Ana and her messenger birds

Just a few seconds, it could not have been longer. And Grandma had reached the open gate and was disappearing through it, unnaturally fast and followed by a cloud of dust. Ed called me again and I ran indoors crossing the wet curtain, not without one last glance at the far-left corner of the "garden" now empty and still.

Beyond the fence boundaries, now the storm raged quite naturally with rhythmic gusts of wind. I was drenched crossing the patio." You will catch your death Ana, out in that weather for an hour!! " Ed admonished in his tender way.

An hour? I had lost an hour or wasted it, depending on the degree of credibility my account may provoke; a thought I could not yet discuss with Ed. Not before I verified the events with tangible proof, in a different frame of mind.

Ed persisted on my forthcoming pneumonia, but I dismissed any further discussion leading to an argument I could not sustain, for reasons only known to me. I introduced the small talk that married couples develop to perfection, innocuous chatter conducive to nowhere, and a muzzle for acute passions into a bearable constant and a tamer of most wild instincts.

"You look tired. Would you like to have a nap after your medicine or would you rather I read you a chapter of the book I'm working on? "

"The second offer, if you don't mind, but dry yourself first." And we spent the rest of the evening in amiable companionship. We dined and watched a documentary about the Berlin wall and the disintegration of the "iron curtain".

Ana and her messenger birds

So many barriers were falling that had kept people apart; the winds of change were sweeping the dust of old memories. We watched in wonder and agreed that nothing, not even the wall was "cast in stone", nothing lasts forever. That day while our evening followed its course unperturbed, Ed spoke of the little time he had, with a stoicism I had never guessed he possessed during our short marriage; he was, he said, ready to die, that it was the right time, in the right place and with the right person by his side. I swallowed each of his words like poisoned arrows, as I did not dare show my revulsion against such peaceful submission.

That night, once he lay in bed drugged into a sleep, I occupied my temporary bed by the bay window listening to the house sounds; those augmented and multiplied their sources as the night travelled through the small hours. I served a voluntary vigil measuring his breath, listening for painful moans, absorbing the storm outside, feeling the rain beat against the beach below. If I could only understand what was happening to me. Cancer could be explained to the layperson, it can be seen through a microscope working his way up tissue and bone and organs but what was dying within me had no physical proportions, no apparent beginning, no foreseeable end.

The storm was affecting me.

I watched over Ed...and waited for Grandma to come back.

3 A SMALL CONFESSION

The loud disjointed squawking of the seagulls, cormorants and the calls of the oyster catchers were our usual dawn chorus after a storm in their tenacious attempts to breakfast off the sea debris strewn about the shoreline. The edible treasures were left exposed behind the ebbing of each wave, tangled within the purple strands of seaweed. Like beds of strawberries, the sea urchins and mussels dotted those vegetable manes, with occasional interest to the flying eye, bringing a measure of excitement to the calm aftermath of a gale. The air flowed with transparency, with a dustless diaphanous nudity that tinted the coastal ocean of an aquamarine colour, like the sky above.

In mornings like those, a mere thought echoed on desires and innocent ideas appeared sinful.

I opened my eyes to the warming effects of a lemony sun flooding the room, to face the affectionate stare of Ed, who had been observing my sleep and the circling flights of the sea birds. I was not used to that kind of intimacy. Not anymore.

Ana and her messenger birds

"Sorry about the open curtain. Last night I fell asleep watching the storm," was all I said for a morning greeting, remembering that he liked to sleep and wake up in darkness.

"Morning to you as well," he replied with a mischievous glee that put me at ease. We were supposed to wake up at different times, in semi-darkness. I would do it first, scurrying out unnoticed to tie my hair, to reappear later armed with the breakfast tray, then I would pull the curtains open and would wake him up…but customs which had eased our past lives into placid natures, had lost the time in which to exist. And neither did we have the inclination now.

"I had never seen your hair loose…and uncombed, my shy siren. Is it naturally curled? "

"I'm afraid most of my relatives had it this way, but I hide it in a knot or a braid. "

"Or under the closed curtains in the mornings…" he suggested adding: " Do you have a large family Ana? "

"No, it's not in the Spanish tradición, small and all women." This said, I quickly disappeared downstairs still in my pyjamas, through the conservatory landing on the patio, with one thought only, on the impulse to look for palpable evidence of her presence there yesterday. And though the morning had the brilliance of a recently finished Canaletto oil painting, "the back" of my house had an opaque layer of dust seemingly deposited over decades of drought and stillness. All colours were sepia tinted. The dust looked pernicious, the soil sterile; all except a patch of ground on the southwest corner near the fence, from which a musty and a sweet aroma oozed to greet the nose. A large hole had been recently dug, unearthing moist soil, generous in worms and other tunnelling creatures that now and again showed their presence around the sloping crevices. A bucket of soil lay by the works. The hole was all of six feet in diameter but shallow.

I went back there a few times before we settled for the afternoon, in the solace of the conservatory but there were neither signs of any unusual presence, nor odd climatic changes.

I began to worry.

Meanwhile, my translation was not running smoothly, and Ed had noticed my mood.

"Are you alright Ana? "

I looked at his preoccupied face, big eyes that had grown bigger as his body lost life. They were darker of late, with a shineless depth of unhealthy origins. His advanced emaciation had exposed his once soft features. Emotions hidden in better days under layers of lustre and good spirits, were revealed in the minimal gesture.

It did pain me to see him unguarded against my eye, vulnerable to the world.

A shadow blurred his eyes when he often looked at me, and his mind would wander to the depths of his dying knowledge. He would forget my presence in contemplation of his very pain, and of some other knowledge he harboured but never shared.

"I'm alright, thanks. " (Though my answer was a hollow reassurance given the new developments in my life).

"Would you say that I was a hysterical woman, you know…

prone to cry, of a nervous disposition, erratic behaviour, imaginings?"

There was a silence of genuine meditation before he admitted defeat.

"I couldn't say. I mean, I have never seen you behaving like one but... I never got to know you Ana, did I? "

"We didn't know each other Ed...but I thought that that had been our mutual aim. That was one of the benefits of our marriage."

"Are the women in your family that way inclined? "

"To marry strangers? "

"To hysterical tendencies. " Ed chastised my flippancy.

"Well, Grandma was a very dramatic character, though solid as a rock, the source of primaeval wisdom and archaic proverbs. She used to bury her troubles in the kitchen but never burnt a single meal. You know...she has been dead for over twenty years and I don't think she is aware of the fact or if she has noticed, I don't think she cares about such an impediment in life."

"And you, Ana? " He asked tentatively, not catching the full meaning of my drift.

"If I care about it? "

"Ana..."

" If I'm like her? Well...it all depends on the implications and inferences that others make of words, their imagery and labels; besides...a good ex-catholic girl should never discuss herself." I knew I was diverting his attention unsuccessfully.

"What do you think was your Grandma's best trait? "

"I think it may have been her capacity to adapt without

great expectations from outcomes."

"And you Ana, did you once have great expectations? "

" No...well, yes I suppose...like every young woman..."

" Why that doubt? "

" Yaya didn't have dreams, ideals, prospects, small chances, an ageing dictator, a romantic aunt, she had no choices, so she never made big mistakes, only small errors of judgement. "

"Was loving him your big mistake? "

" No, it was marrying him. "

"Another stranger? "But Ed instantly apologised for his flippancy.

"I was expecting his child. "

"I never knew you had children!! "

"I don't have them. I have lost my only daughter. " It escaped in a flat monotone.

"How did she die? "

Plop, plop, plop. Someone had pulled the plug and my boat was taking in water. A drowning tide was rising within me. Fifteen years of separation, a decade and a half of wandering solitude, of her absent laughter, and the not-knowing whether she had happily forgotten me... (or dreading it) were sinking in the nebulousness of my emerging pain. Memories, which I had never tried recalling, had remained intact and preserved in time without the distortion of daily usage and they had sprung out of my past with pristine clarity and precision, at the invitation of a trusted voice.

They hurt as recent wounds.

"My daughter didn't die. Aurora was taken from me when

she was five years old and I haven't seen her for a very long time. "

I paused gasping for air, to ease the obstruction in my throat but it only made the tide flow easier, on quiet waves of tears. Oh, it is very wrong and unhealthy to let memories simmer so long in the recesses of a broken heart!

My precious daughter.

I rushed to the living room window and opened it to let the Atlantic breeze dry my past, to escape, to merge with that liquid body that also bathes the Spanish shores. The ocean rested exhausted after yesterday's storm, lolling its surface against the polished pebbles with lame undulations.

My days had been succeeding each other sideways, in a fruitless litany of years riding over the horizon line, with an abyss ahead of me and a precipice behind.

I felt Ed wheeling his way towards me, stopping beside me, and holding my hand with his able one.

I drew the horizon line with my right index, in an optical illusion.

"I keep thinking that my daughter is over there and that if I were to touch the same waters bathing both countries, I might fill her life pulsating …. somewhere in Spain.

"You would like to see her. " Ed voiced my hopeless wish.

"She will be twenty-five this October. A young woman who has most probably forgotten her mother ...to my regret though not to hers, I hope."

I wheeled Ed back to the conservatory and began the prologue of my long-awaited disclosures.

"You found unnecessary, during our marriage, all the

secrecy which made perfect strangers of us, but you see....
We had never been anything else...and but a few
disagreements over it, what you didn't know couldn't hurt
you. "

"Then, why now? "

"I have this feeling: it isn't only you who approaches the day
of reckoning. Whatever might befall you, will also touch me
reverberating long passed our days. You see, I did learn to
love you. Gone are the days when I believed I could steer my
life along the route of my choosing. It is of late that I began
to feel the weight of time, and to notice that all I have done
is run against the pulling forces of circumstance. And that
tidal movement is keeping us swimming frantically towards
the beach, where we are thrust irrevocably deeper into the
open seas...buffeted, and by now Ed, I wish to reach dry
land before I exhaust the life I have learnt to love against all
odds. I wish for the peace I see around, but I cannot
conquer. I long to sleep without nightmares. I yearn for my
unutterable wish to come to pass and stay with me. "

"All this because you are the witness of my daily decline! "
Ed uttered ruefully.

"All this because you came back here, not just to me but the
familiar, to your past and to what you consider important to
say farewell to while I am so far away from mine. "

"I know Ana that nothing is more important than living,
when one is dying. "

"There is Ed. It is living with whom you love. It is not
missing a human being every conscious hour. The days grow
colder without shared memories to fuel them. It is not to

depart from this life a pariah, without luggage, no mementoes or tacky souvenirs to cling to. It's not to waste a life by keeping it empty and barren. "

"I never suspected that side of you. "

"What side of me?" I asked but he maintained the suspense and I allowed his tacit bartering, a question for a question and an answer for another. It had brought colour to his cheeks.

I realised then that disclosing my past might alleviate his present…as well as mine.

4 A SUDDEN MARRIAGE

Who I was and who I had been, I had not yet attempted to decipher; a heavy collection of mummified ghosts, unanswered questions and sentimental artefacts in my past had created a wall more than a decade ago, behind which I had haphazardly stored myself, deep in the recesses of the mind, with the intention of avoiding the hurt.

Events had not been catalogued in any order, a lifetime had not been analysed and reasons had not been reasoned. But if Ed had answered my question, would his answer have pleased me?

But who was better qualified to judge me than myself, who possessed all the evidence?

During a heated argument twenty-five years ago, I put that question to my mother, who could not suffer human erring with equanimity. And I had erred most abominably against her beliefs.

"What kind of woman do you think I am? " I asked her, still with the pride of innocence, with my metal still resisting her moral hammering. And mother had retorted with that acute tongue that the bible had exquisitely sharpened through long reading and extensive use of its muscles:

"You know what you are, Madame? You are pregnant! Not a decent young girl anymore, nor a respectable married mother. No! You are just pregnant, and the consequence of your fall will live forever, growing as big as yourself, to remind us all of what you once were.

"Pregnant!!"

"You can't mean to be so cruel, mother."

"And you, did you mean to fall so low in pursuit of your aunt's fancy ideas? Did you mean to soil my name? "

That Sunday evening, the hot chocolate cups and Sunday confectionery traditionally arranged (as every Sunday afternoon and Holy days) over doilies and plates, on the laced tablecloth, were shaking by the vibrations of my mother's anger and disappointment. The clock on the Colonial dresser had stopped. Its pendulum had recoiled within its casing in fear and the cream in the milk jug had begun to curdle. Our well-polished and seldom visited parlour had never housed such commotion. I was the daughter God had punished her with, the instrument of her penance for deeds she would never expose. I tried to reason my point with her, to bridge the chasm long time carved between us and offered various solutions avoiding the expected wedding but, " I had inflicted my sins onto her and had wounded her, The Saint Mother Church, every God fearing creature and our God of all things chaste".

Reparations were due, expected, demanded.

I must state that I was not forced to marry but…during the

two months that lapsed between my admission and the wedding, maternal coercion reached sublime heights and painful displays of pathos.

Until the said time of my loss of virtue, mother had lived an isolated existence gravitating between the sepulchral twilight of her bedroom, the church, and the polished furniture at home. She had, during my childhood, relinquished all earthly pleasures and duties and entrusted me to my aunt, for her better acquaintance with God. "One could always rely on Him because He was universally right and dependable", she used to say when challenged about her beatitude.

Flesh and meat being all the same, mother gave them up the day my father deserted us; though through the years she had conducted her malaise unobtrusively, within a domesticity parallel to our own. Mother did not evangelise to those beyond remission.

However, my state had disturbed her sanctity. She suffered fits and migraines and went about the house in penitent recitation of her Rosary, downcast and pale. The bible she had constantly quoted became part of her hand's anatomy, like her rings and fingers and she turned into my shadow, wherever I chose to sit reciting, murmuring, and prophesying eternal damnation.

Antonio, my then boyfriend and father of my predicament, came home on leave that October weekend, for a long weekend once his basic training was completed. He was serving his conscription, the first of some unwanted fifteen months but as things turned out, he never finished his recruitment.

Ana and her messenger birds

Mother had surreptitiously sought reinforcements and found an eager ally in Antonio. There must have been some correspondence between them because that weekend, each sentence flowed from one to the other for completion, as if the two shared one mind; when the most charitable feeling they had for each other was indifference in the best of times.

Together, they massaged the wedding theme with dexterity over the Sunday tea; however, on that occasion the commotion was contained within ourselves and mother's rage restrained to just the tapping of fingers on the delicate filigree of the table-cloth. The hot chocolate was growing cold in the cups, its surface forming a wrinkled skin that grew thicker as the plot around them developed a surreal magnitude.

Somehow, word of his impending fatherhood had reached the captain's ears and those, being of impeccable nature, were ringing with echoes of dishonour into the purer receptacles of the army chaplain. A legal reparation was due while serving conscription and failure to do so (unless the expectant mother refused the offer), carried a jail sentence.

I refused his offer.

Mother begged him not to divulge my wantonness.

Antonio proposed a second time.

I said we did not love each other.

He cupped my hand on his own across the table." Marry me Ana."

I... thought of my aunt and her books, her heroes and heroines; that warmth my aunt maintained existed when real love had brought a couple together, that yearning for the mere contact of hands......

"Marry him Ana", mother expostulated.

I was not given to regrets. I did not regret my fatherless life, my mother's absence from it, neither did I regret the mess I was in, nor disturbing the peace of those who were keeping my country down... but I regretted him.

A black moth had landed on my heart.

Dark wings of an inconclusive thought.

With the flitting shadow of a bad augur.

And the dignity of youth prevailing....

I refused his offer again.

All the years of strict indoctrination had not dented my aunt's labouring care. What seed mother had sown by dogma, Aunt Celia had turned sterile with her generous example. I could recite the entire catechism with Jesuitical zeal but deadly indifference, while the lecture of any of my aunt's books moved me to heights as none of Father Tomas' sermons had ever done.

Mother landed her right fist on the table upsetting the buoyancy of the wrinkled chocolate skin and said, grinding her words as they came out in big lumps, that " she might as well die there and then rather than share the shame of her unmarried daughter. So, Antonio offered solicitously to refuse to marry me and save me the shame of doing it...."No matter how heavy the sentence. It could not be longer than five years. ``

That was a bluff I could not call out. If my senses were mistaken, I could be responsible for the future of many. I looked around for help, but this was a censored meeting, no aunt or Grandma to support me.... And he looked sincere in his hour of martyrdom. Perhaps he was doing what was expected of him in the circumstances. It might have been that he loved me in a manner I was yet to feel or...something else. I could not decipher the riddle.

He had appeared in town one day for one job or another, keeping any particulars of himself and his family private, in romantic anonymity, and I at twenty, had not been interested in those matronly affairs. He was enigmatic, outlandish with his cut and dry accent from Madrid. Who needed more details? We had been just playing, no harm meant. The regime was softening, the Dictator, very old.

We were sure to inherit a freed country soon, with prospects and dreams but I...would not be a bird of that paradise. I was being expelled from it by my own volition. I looked at Antonio and mother alternatively, their chocolate cups in hand, suspended in mid-air, eyes inscrutable in their own different depths...

I consented to the wedding.

We were married three days later, with a special licence granted by his regiment's captain. There was no banquet to celebrate the occasion, no guests to ponder at the urgency of the affair and no man in my family to give me away. Antonio's friend and my aunt were our witnesses. Aunt Celia, who had not wanted me married, was my only witness. My mother remained at home with one of her turns and Gramma stayed behind, "in case..." My husband was discharged from the army the day after he went back to barracks as a marital law for conscripts demanded. The state absolved from his duties any man with dependents on him.

I learnt later …sadly too late.

I stopped my narrative there, when I involuntarily arrived at the conclusions I should have reached some years ago. I had been a pawn in my new husband's game. Ed was silent. The ocean outside was quiet and the breeze that usually hissed its way around the house walls from the beach below, had ceased to murmur its age-old tunes. It was comforting to share the quiet understanding of my dreadful mistake. I had wondered for twenty-five years, searched for that particular set of circumstances which had thrown us together and pushed us apart, unaware of the hand that had forced events, while in the process life had drifted by me unlived.

Ed and I remained silent for a while longer, watching the moon emerge from the right of the living room window, new and fat; while the sun dived beneath the western side of our promontory and the remains of its red halo tinted the evening. That double act of moon and sun unique to our position in the small peninsula illuminated our still unlit intimacy, turning sepia every colour in the living room and conservatory.

"This is a magical place to live in, Ana" Ed confessed and added " The best to die in also. Thanks for letting me stay."

I took him upstairs in silence and helped him into our former bed. Dinner had become a tray affair in those days, to facilitate his nightly medicinal ritual before bedtime. The canker consuming his life could not be seen but its effects were creeping in inexorably. From a sick but able man a few weeks ago, Ed had deteriorated so much as to need the installation of that ubiquitous lift chair.

 He was slowly dying.

And his departure would pass unnoticed to his God, who was keeping a low profile during his ordeal and yet ...my ex-husband would not question his "fait-accompli."

Sitting by the side of my sentinel's bed in the darkened room, I watched him sleep feeling myself fettered to events I had no control over. His life was pattering to a halt, alas! now when we were reaching a timid understanding.

Ed had had a benign influence in my life, I reflected with regret, and regretted the memories of our acquaintance, which I had neglected to cultivate. Seeing his placid shape, I wondered where that God of his was. What disaster would shake him out of his complacency and what evil deeds had Ed been accused of, to deserve a foretold end; when there are malevolent people parading their unhindered longevity, to whom death might come swiftly and unannounced.

 " Why don't you help him out?"

I asked aloud about me...and nothing. There was no answer within me, neither the echoes of it in the sound of thunder or some unexplained phenomenon. Calm reigned about me, in the spectral grey drags and silver strands of the contents that bedrooms have at night-time, in those amorphous shapes that borrow the appearance of bad dreams. Nothing.

A blasphemy or two passed my lips to no avail. Nothing.

I might have bargained for his life if there had been the response of a supreme will, but I stood there alone between his faith and the nothingness of death, determined to fill in the gaps of his moribund conscience. I would be his hands and legs when they all fail, I would be his happiness, his life if necessary…if necessary, I would construct his peace over my own ruins.

Thus determined, I fell in an all-repairing slumber, of which I only remember parts of a dream unrelated to the day's events: I was on a sleeper train, travelling through a Valencian landscape I had never seen before, carpeted with orange groves to the right and a set of mountains to the left. I was sitting at a table in the restaurant coach, having breakfast. The waiter had brought me the bill and I went to look for my purse inside my bag, when a kitchen knife fell from it to the floor, to which he said, "You will not be needing that Señora."

5 CAROLINA

We had awakened in a Sunday mood (the best) and were greeted by a promising day. The church at the centre of the village hillside peeled its song with languor. Its Norman tower spread the recorded notes that had decanted downhill for centuries, with the same pulling power, if not similar results in attendance.

Outside, about the neatly packed vicinity and down-hill roads, a buzzing noise began to materialise after breakfast; not the speedy clamour of a weekday but that simple sound of Sundays' routines only audible when the pace of life slows down, freed from paid labour.

There was a soft chatter and patter from visiting relatives up and down the hill, to and from the newsagent, the church and sporadic trips to the beach below us, by adults laden with children and dogs in summer spirits.

It was definitely a day for gardening undertakings and to that purpose I left Ed, comfortably reading on the patio, to work around the garden; though my euphoria evaporated at the sight of browning flower beds, foliage turned brittle like old papyrus from one day to the next. I sighed in dismay and Ed followed my stare noticing the obvious.

"Didn't you plant bluebells two years ago, Ana?"

"These are them," I pointed at the strands of raffia strewn across the flower beds." And these here were the Lavender and over there on the right are the skeletons of my poor Lavatera trees".

"Are you sure you know what you are doing Ana? "

"That's beside the point. Haven't you noticed the blight around us? It has nothing to do with my care and skills. It's as if a sinister will is feeding off the sap as soon as I bed it in."

"Probably some deficiency in the soil." He put it tentatively.

"Or …a lack of green fingers." I said casually.

"I see you feel better today."

"Better than those bluebells, I think".

"Well now, would you like to tell us the secrets of gardening?" I demanded defiantly, daring him to deliver.

"…Ashes…"

"Pardon?"

"Ashes are the Rosetta stone."

"Are they? Do you mean my smoking was beneficial after all?"

"It's the fire, you know. It works wonders. It purifies. It produces instant potassium. A new life comes out of the pyre."

"Not to the poor Indian widow! " And I sat near his wheelchair vaguely aware of where our conversation was sliding towards.

"I will make a bonfire after lunch, then."

"When my time comes, I would like to be cremated, Ana. Will you spread my ashes around your garden?"

A strange bond was growing around our estrangement. A need for the carefree closeness of summer friends without neither past nor future perspectives to fear. (A traveller waits for his train at the station and sits on an already occupied bench, so those two strangers exchange experiences and unload their troubles onto the other, in the knowledge that their paths will never cross again and they part, and they travel lighter to their destinations).

"I can't be your widow, Ed, when I don't even know what I am. What we are to each other."

"We can be friends... the best of friends."

And as such we exchanged gardening tips and anecdotes, while the few scattered clouds of the morning piled up and mushroomed gliding across the blue, westwards. The breeze that propelled them thus, could be heard hissing an old tune:

"There are women like fires....

...Consuming passion that expires......"

It was hard to ignore that rancid melody.

"You never mentioned your family Ed."

"My brother died five years ago."

"Is that why you..."

"Why did I marry you? Yes. He was my last relative. I was left alone to bear the loss... and loneliness is a poor companion for the mourning heart. Spain was the furthest I could get from my memories with the minimum of effort and then…I saw your advert in the embassy's newsletter seeking temporary accommodation and a crazy idea gained weight when I heard your voice and reasons on the phone. You were alone in the world and wanted a break. I was lonely. Marriage would bring us companionship, a new beginning (here he paused to engage my eyes) …but I grew to love you in silence, desperately. It was not supposed to happen but for the very fact that you were an intriguing riddle to me, passionate but distant your smile never reached your eyes."

Forbidden images accumulated above us in the cottony clouds.

"Am I still a riddle to you? "

"Now we don't share a bed, my Ana." He blandly slipped in the comment, so I let it slip further, unheard into oblivion while I brought the gardening theme back.

I built a bonfire. The wooden corpses burned easily, with crackling noises and sparkling bursts that excited our attention. Wood fires had always captivated me. Even Ed 's more prosaic nature fell under the spell. Every spark and undulation of the flames sent us deeper within ourselves.

Time came and went in that state of contemplation.

"What are you thinking, Ed? "

"Of our years together and apart, and you? "

"Of other fires, childhood fires burned for San Antón, the patron saint of animals in Spain. Those could reach dangerous proportions in the narrow streets of my native town. During the evening of that date each year, in most streets, every neighbour helped to build a bonfire contributing with a broken chair, a termite ridden headboard or Christmas tree, which would be left burning to embers, allowing time for young and old to gather around it to pole-vault it, to play by its warmth, to dream by its magical side, to meditate in the darkness of its wake, to talk...to gossip about the interim year in grandiloquent terms and epic summaries...to roast sweet potatoes.

During the early burning in which the flames illuminated the identities of the speakers, the general conversation floated in short tirades of harmless teasing and banter between neighbours. Women and children, men and youths all interrupting each other with more important or funnier anecdotes. When familiarity brought more intimacy and the receding flames allowed a more adventurous dialogue, when the lateness of the hour lent anonymity to all within; then the circle would thin out as some retired while the rest gathered in small groups. It was then that men spoke in whispers, uttered well-known subversive truisms, and political rhetoric. It was then when grandmothers narrated incredibly gruesome stories of anticipated strict morals, to avid little childhood ears all agog. And it was at that time that youths dared each other to pole-vault the smouldering embers for the girls' sake. And the women...well, the women exchanged vital secrets and passed judgement on other women, life, society, the decaying morals, men, other women's progeny, cookery recipes, husbands, in-laws...life again....

Chicory coffee was passed around by the gallon until the early hours of the morning, when without ceremony, sand was thrown over the dying embers before breaking up the party. Then as quickly as the affair was put together, it dissolved.

Like every other child present in those gatherings, I decoded the secret language in which each group conversed, but I never used it because the death of the General made the game irrelevant. At a certain point of a conversation, " have you left the clothes on the line " will prop up and the meaning of words clouded over, though adults appear to understand what was being said…"

Memories, memories!

The rot of an empty carcass.

Past echoes were creeping out of the safe box where I stored them, when I came to England as a bride five years ago. Other mementoes of my life with Ed escaped as well, as I observed him lost in thoughts of his own memorabilia. I touched his shoulder to bring him round. We were going to get wet. The cloud that had been gathering above us all day was now seriously laden and leaking through. A flash, some thunder and before we could reach cover, its underbelly burst open with fury.

We observed the hypnotic fall pelting the different surfaces of the patio absorbing the magic of that stormy dusk. The eye grew accustomed to the increasing darkness and the dense screen of water when…Oh dear! I perceived a darker and mobile shape on the far-left corner of the garden. Once again!

I ran to the garden on an impulse saying to Ed that I had to secure the back gate. Outside, the bonfire was just a pile of wet ashes sipping into the soil. I crossed the rain curtain expectantly, proceeding through the same path, retracing with meticulous detail the movements and thoughts of the first time and repeating them like a ritual, wishing for the apparition to materialise a second time, for the spell to be cast.

Once in the centre of the garden, the rain was no more around me, though the thicket of the storm obliterated the out-shape of my home.

In contrast, a timid setting sun bathed the left corner and there, by the fence, was Gramma digging, her skirts pinned up from the back to the front of her waistband, between her legs, in a trouser like fashion long forgotten.

A second spade lay by her side. I picked it up and commenced my aimless digging close to her.

She smiled, lifting her left eyebrow in a conspiring gesture and all the black of her attire could not hide the brightness of her spirit.

"The back gate was opened, Anita. You should be more careful."

And she resumed her digging, pushing her spade deep into the soil, pressing it with her left wooden clog to bring out a clump of rich soil and archaic humus and did it again…and again.

"We don't want undesirables to see what we are digging."

"What are we digging for, Yaya?" I asked, dying of curiosity.

"Don't you know? " And she tutted with reproach." Your grandfather never knew whether he was coming or going on many an unfortunate occasion as well." Gramma maintained the conversation as we worked. " Never knew it until it was too late to rectify… too late to plead for his life. My knees still hurt from kneeling. When I remember…but our prayers fell on deaf ears. A hard lot they were!"

"Who? " I asked.

Gramma glanced at me, through me, past me… and started in sombre tones. "We were caught between the fortifications of Bilbao and the advancing Nationals from the East of Guernica, an April day like this one fifty three years ago. Our defending troops were in retreat and had split in three. Some were heading for the mountains, a second group marched west to protect Bilbao and a third formed of Communist and Republican militiamen and women came to Guernica.

Where the fighting factions went and whatever side they stood for; they invariably arrived in populated areas and organised the immediate recruitment of every useful man, to help their cause until they moved on or back…and the next faction moved in. No man was allowed to stand aside and avoid the conflict.

Victor, your grandfather, was made to volunteer on account of the old "Hispano" automobile we had parked in the courtyard gathering dust and he was instructed to drive up to Bilbao. A British merchant ship called " The Seven Seas Spray " had broken the nationalist blockade, entering the mouth of the river Nervión. Your grandfather was given Communist gasoline and issued with Republican money, to bring munitions and victuals, all pre-arranged and waiting for collection.

Your granddad came back from his errand two days later and handed it over to the Captain of the R. squadron, with the additional booty of another less fortunate messenger caught in a skirmish by the roadside and left to die, protecting a cargo which wasn't his to die for. That particular officer took my Victor's generosity for what it was: a bribe to release a man from his duties, and as he was a connoisseur of human nature, and knew that this prevails unharnessed when hunger drowns our better principles, he had him followed to find the rest of the flour cargo. Transacted in the usual place, that dusty contraband might have yielded one month's wages, but he was apprehended inside the church of Saint Prosperous, with twenty kilos of flour packed in brown paper bags.

At this stage, Gramma crouched and curled herself within her body, covering her face with the corners of her multifaceted black apron, sobbing half a century of guilt. She was no more the fortress of my infancy, rather a defeated old woman whose heartache pricked mine.

I sat by her, not daring to touch her shivering form, afraid that my contact might have conjured up reality.

"What did they do to Grandfather? " I asked to stop her from disintegrating amidst our tears.

She dried her face and blew her nose with her apron to proceed with her story. "Padre Miguel was shot in the aisle and his fall reverberated long after the dust had settled over the saints that from their alcoves watched the scene with stony calm. Only the dust had stirred. It floated for a while round his inert body, to create a false aura against the light traversing the leaded windows at either side of the altar. The church had been closed for two weeks, to remain so for the duration of the war, for fear of communist vandalism but Padre Miguel had been keeping business as usual.

He was left there, alone with the Lord and twenty kilos of flour spread over the floor when he fell. His blood thickened by the spilled flour and the flour bloodied as the two mingled in the spillage. And your grandfather… he was taken to the Jesuit school in the old quarter. There he was to be tried and shot. Never trust "the black army" of our lord. They betrayed their own and their countrymen; they were so eager to side with whoever was in charge.

When I received the news of his fate, I had just one hour in which to arrange every detail…for all eventualities…to hold destiny's most favourable hand. During that fateful hour…

…I killed Pepa our laying hen,
Laid her on a bed of rosemary
In the market basket…and then,
I proceeded to enhance my attributes
(Should the need arise) …and then,
Collected our last eggs and blankets
Under the stairs' room…and then,
Our three daughters followed in
For safekeeping…and then,
Bestowed heirlooms upon the oldest
(Might never the chance) …and then
Locked my heart within that cupboard;
Should the need arise…and then,
I slid the key under its door….
For it might be of use to them…
…………………… after all.

Ana and her messenger birds

And I ran to beg for his reprieve.

My journey was a hazardous race through the " Via del Norte", negotiating the waves of pedestrians and traffic that were converging in the spacious street, from every road and alleyway. The vehicles hooted at the tanks rolling in short convoys, while the cyclists had taken to the already crowded pavements. The fleeing multitude cried, shouted, trampled, and held on to the small ones but never once lent a glance to the retreating Republican 12 Battalion leaving town with the civilians. Their concern was to avoid being left behind, on foot, between two armies.

I left that beehive swarming towards the surrounding fields of west Guernica and made for the Jesuit school, where the rear-guard of the Communist flank was hard at work, to see that no traitor could run too soon to welcome the incoming Nationalist saviours.

Men's ideals!!!

Of your grandfather, I only saw a mass of limbs tangled and mangled in a bloody pile, as the militia began to fill in the ditch, hurriedly, before the coming offensive might deviate them from their duty. Their unswerving dedication had frozen their humanity. They performed their duties with relish; unaware of the dozen or so widows that watched the ritual with broken hearts.

Men's ideals!!!

Young and old widows, we all huddled together hopelessly holding an array of baskets, of which we didn't have use for anymore. We looked on, whispering our Lord's prayer once…twice…and many times over while the ditch was being filled with bodies and stones and guns and soil, and the last days of security for us all present, perpetrators and victims.

The militiamen went to join their comrades when their job was done, leaving no trace of the killing. An hour or so, a dozen or so corpses and a dozen or so widows and mothers; so little time used to create such everlasting destruction… but back then, we didn't feel the enormity of our loss because the tremors of the bombings over the eastern hills urged us to run to our cupboards full of daughters.

So, I ran…and ran like Peter the apostle.

Once in the safety of the old town's alleyways, freed from the tumultuous crowds of wider streets and protected by the shadows of converging rooftops, I transferred the sachet of our life savings from the bottom of my negotiating basket, to the intimate pocket in my petticoat and then started a brisk march home, eager and apprehensive… and ashamed of my determination to survive, to flee south".

"And my Victor was still warm."

Gramma fell silent, in shameful silence. Her eyes wandered over the fence, across the ocean; her closely ploughed face darkened under the remembered ghosts that plagued her purgatory, as they danced a macabre waltz. She reached for her pocket and took out a gold pendant locket, which she held tight while she uttered a long, blasphemous tirade, intended to offend the coarsest of men…. I gasped in dismay and looked around us for any unfortunate ear while she used that opportunity and slipped away through the back gate, leaving her locket behind, by the ever-growing hole. I snatched it and ran towards the rain curtain, to the familiar sound of Ed's voice hoping, like all grave robbers, that the dead would forgive me.

I had no means of knowing how long I had been outdoors; whether time had passed or just stood still beyond life. However, Ed did not seem concerned but for the weather and what such escapades might do to my health. I tried to appease him but how could I explain what I could not understand myself?

The locket felt cold to my touch. I opened it carefully, forcing its minute hinges to uncover a triptych gallery of miniature portraits in sepia colours. Its central figure was that of a teenage girl, whose angular face and dark hair were eerily familiar. The pictures of my Aunt Celia and mother in their twenties flanked and completed the meaning of the triple relic, and though the virtues and flaws of the older two were not identical, their likeness to the central portrait twinned them. Was that girl the third daughter of Gramma's story? But why hadn't I been told about her? …. What tragedies had impeded her rest, I wondered?

I handed the jewel to Ed, who was oblivious to these happenings. He studied the portraits, the nameless central face particularly so.

"I can see the family resemblance in them. Is this your daughter in the middle?"

"That…. I think it might have been my other aunt. I now believe she died during the war."

"The second war? Ed was intrigued, curious, quite revived.

Ana and her messenger birds

"Of course not, our war, the Spanish civil war. It must be hard for those who can't lay that past to rest because they can't find it!" I was thinking of my grandma and some imaginary events that might be keeping her from her resting place.

"And you Ana, can you lay yours to rest? "

The living should not need to lay the past to rest.

"And Ana can't live with hers?"

"Ana's past is full of skeletons and riddles Ed." And with this I began to switch on all lights and lamps, to dispel our penumbra, to vanish ghosts to the confines of my universe, but they seem to move alongside me, like my own shadow. I asked Ed about his headache, and he reckoned that the storm had eased his aches and pains…but the weight of past and present memories was not alleviated, turning the air heavy, unbreathable.

"How are your leg and arm feeling?"

"They are cold, deadly cold." And a grip tightened in my chest, as it had become a frequent occurrence in my conscious hours.

"Let me give you a massage to ease your blood circulation." And to that effect I collected the necessary aromatic oils, tissues and good will, and arranged our chairs to facilitate my work. Side by side, his left and my right knee touching. I then rolled up his left sleeve and brought his inert hand to rest on my lap. The inadequacy of the arrangement became obviously awkward…awkwardly obvious. I had not been trained as a nurse to perform in sensitive circumstances, nor was I adept to deal with sensations I was not supposed to feel. My skin vibrated under the subtle contact and the spontaneity of that shared pleasure blighted our studied camaraderie because…his hand had been there before. Ed suppressed a chuckle when I changed the offending limb to his own lap, and he deposited it over my lap again with his other hand.

"No feelings in this hand, remember?"

I remembered… and the tension lessened. The magic around his dormant limb was dispelled. It was no longer an instrument of love but the reminder of his coming death. I retrieved the folly within myself, neatly folded between the layers of my good reasoning and resumed the massage. Ed let his eye wander disinterestedly about the room until my work on the table caught it. He picked it with his right and began flicking through the pages, stopping at some curious paragraph for a while.

"You don't say that you are actually reading."

"I am. " He returned jovially and proceeded to read the manuscript aloud with a soft accent of timid "Rs" and ambiguous vowels.

"I didn't know you spoke Spanish that well!"

"I never thought you a Florence Nightingale either! "

"Did you think me insensitive to your suffering?"

"Do you care what I think of you nowadays, Ana? " (of course, I did)

Ah… the questioning game in which I was a reluctant player…but Ed pressed on ingeniously.

"What type of woman would you say you are, Ana?"

"How can I answer my own riddle? "

"Who else if not oneself? Unless that is, one dies; then you may have an obituary, but eulogies aren't what you are after my Ana, you are looking for the truth..."

"If my past were my witness…"

"You sound extremely operatic…"

"Dramas are dramatic."

"And memories fade beneath the cobwebs…"

"Doesn't the truth prevail past our time? "

"How can it ever exist if it's never told, Ana?"

"Some awful deeds are branded in the memory, indelibly bright. "

"You are not responsible for the actions of others. "

"It's what I didn't do that will be my undoing."

"And you don't want to be reminded? "

"Dear me! I just wish that this perpetual cloud gravitating over me would disperse and let me see the sunlight. There is a constant grip around my chest nowadays, " I said, holding his hand to it as a natural extension of speech.

"I can't feel your heart Ana." Our eyes met." You could cut it or cup your breast in it, and I wouldn't feel the pain or pleasure. This numbness augurs death, you know. Better to feel your hurt than this nothingness." And with his other hand he caressed my face, tracing my lips. I moved from my chair to his lap and hid my sorrow in the collar of his shirt, and in that fashion, we played at being gay and whole, and in love.

That night I read him a passage from two of the books Ed concurrently enjoyed, with the intention (as he put it) to deceive time with such duplicity, until he fell asleep cocooned in the warmth of half a dozen hot water bottles. His fifty-something face reverted to the happy Ed of happier times, while he slept unaware of my contemplation. Something stirred within me, yawned, and woke up. A flicker yet too small to melt the ice sheet enveloping my emotions, but certain enough to crack it in various floating icebergs.

6 AUNT CELIA

"Monday and Tuesday will be unusually warm for mid-April, with blue skies until the next weather front reaches the Southwest on Tuesday evening", had said the over-enthusiastic voice of the weatherman. The Gods of good fortune smiled at us when the Atlantic currents behaved as predicted and the weather reporter would be quoted and respected for the next few days, whilst we, (weather permitting) felt rewarded for the trust we bestowed upon his strange love of failure.

Spring was a month old, and our spirits, tempered by the fair weather, had found the same wavelength. Solitude could never be loneliness again when it was shared, and the weather was warm.

I had wheeled Ed out to the "back" wrapped in a travelling blanket, to enjoy our April wonder, armed with a bucket, trowel and gardening book, each of us with a straw hat and the ardent desire to resuscitate our moribund garden. I left him in the centre of it, from where he read to me very loud,

following my every movement with the zeal of an amateur."
To improve your drainage, raise your flower beds and add
grit." " You could use the soil dug out of that hole by the left
corner, said Ed." So, I collected the soil from Gramma's
work on the west side and transported it to the right corner.
The fence there worked as a retaining wall against the sloping
hill above, from which the entire house plot had been carved.
" You dig a hole twice as large as the root ball, spread
compost liberally and water the hole before planting. Did you
buy any compost Ana? Listen here: "bone meal and blood" is
a good fertiliser. It sounds gruesome. Are we feeding
sharks?"

"We might produce carnivorous fuchsias."

"Or killer tomatoes," I said bursting into laughter.

Ed was showing interest in the different names of plants I
had bought, interest I could not satisfy ignorant as I was of
the vegetable world; so he went back to the gardening
manual: "(Herbaceous plants are better planted in Autumn).
Me thinks that we are a bit late for all these plants. (Most
spring flowering plants are best bedded in Autumn and
dormant tubers which have been stored away through Winter
should be planted out when there is no danger of frosts)
Blast!!! " Ed exclaimed in dismay, closing the book with a
sonorous crashing of pages." We are too late to revive this
wasteland! " But he continued more sheepishly. " I won't live
to see the dahlias planted."

"Yes, you will. I shall plant climbers, bushes, evergreens,
herbaceous and tubers and any plant courageous enough to
survive this present desert, and you shall see it become an

oasis and the bloom will dazzle you ... and their scent will inebriate your blood. You keep reading to me and I'll work at it."

And I laboured at the pace of his reading until lunchtime, which consisted (as the easiest food to handle with one hand) of sandwiches. While Ed had his nap, I phoned Mr. Lawrence at the publishers in London to request my long overdue holiday, then I went back outdoors laden with the last tray of rosemary and lavender plants, tip-toeing across the patio where he slept reclined in my deck chair. His forbidding wheelchair lay empty at his left side, his face hidden under the straw hat, his thoughts...rested, and the afternoon was sliding westwards noiselessly but for a tenuous breeze that perturbed the otherwise indolent tableau, with echoes of that old tune:

"There are women like flowers,

Whose' death will be for ours "

The garden gate at the far end was open. I left the patio for the garden to close it, experiencing a sudden drop in the temperature. That earlier breeze had turned to wind shaking the spindly trunks of my recently planted saplings. The cherry tree I had planted in the morning matured as I approached it. Its leaves turned reddish brown and brittle, and were plucked by an unnatural autumnal wind as I advanced, to fall on the now sodden soil by my right. The virginia creeper had covered all its allocated space in the retaining fence with burnt orange leaves, and the Russian vine had spread its now tired branches all over the spaces left available, threatening an imminent invasion of the hillside above it. A climatological translocation was taking grip around me. Under the now bare pear tree in the centre of the garden, where I was intending to bed the rosemary I was still carrying in my hands, there stood a woman, in her forties, tall and oddly familiar, scattering bread crumbs for a hungry flock of crows waiting on the barren branches. The woman turned to look at my plants and commented with cheek and knowledge; " That rosemary will look and grow better under the retaining fence, facing south, all along that bed. Don't you think Ana? Woodland plants will look more natural under trees."

The features of her face had never changed but her body stooped slightly forward, hiding her unusual height or as she used to put it, "Her back couldn't hold the weight of her generous front ". She was my aunt. My new visitor was the heroine of my childhood, defender of lost causes and my unconditional ally, a devoted daughter and doting aunt, and the spinster of our family. There (in the Spain of my childhood), had been families that owned a pedigree dog, others had a drunkard, and the least of them had a relative who was found hanging from some beam, but we had had auntie Celia...who had made of spinsterhood, a desirable profession against social and religious adversity. She had been like a mother to me, but not quite, like a friend to all the children in my street... but not quite so. Aunt Celia became a renowned spinster but not quite so much a spinster as a "single woman", agreed most neighbours at the time. This was an accolade because the term only existed in the Hollywood fantasy world; in the Spain of the regime, a single woman in possession of a happy temperament and some means was an unknown quantity feared by men, mistrusted by women and condemned by the church. She had been a singular woman, single minded and with the single intention to do good, because she was good, and all knew it.

And now, something was troubling her beyond the grave. She kneeled and began to plant bulbs of all kinds and sizes from the wicker basket she had nearby. I also knelt and helped her to position a pail of pebbles by handing them one by one into her expert hands.

"I collected them on the beach down below." were the only sounds she emitted for quite a while.   Together we filled the ground under the pear tree with future splendour, and then moved on to plant my lavender. The weather was closing in. Time seemed of vital importance to her that had none at all in which to dwell. Her attention veered constantly from our surroundings to the skies, checking the developments in both, as if she knew of an impending disaster, of a nature too awful to contemplate, of which I was unaware. My intrigue turned to apprehension when she, having surveyed the grounds, reached the far-right corner between the retaining fence and the back gate, and went down on her fours. She began tapping each of the egg-sized stones, lifting them from the ground and inspecting the holes they left behind.

"What are you looking for?" I asked very, very alarmed.

"Scorpions."

"Yellow scorpions? "

"What else? We'll make sure you don't have a nasty

encounter, not deadly mind you…but their sting hurts for a very long time. Look!! " She had found one under a stone and expertly trapped its body under its own cover, rendering its tail limp, which she then took between her index and thumb, releasing the body from its trap. A body that frantically twisted and turned in mid-air sequestered by its tail, until she deposited it on the reverse of her left hand, where the creature stood immobile. Aunt Celia lifted her hand close to her face, and both met in deadly silence. She weighed the passive animal pensively and put it back in his hole.

"Our fear is our only handicap Ana. All the while you are unduly afraid but so it is, and the sting won't last forever. "

"Were you ever stung by one of them Tita? "

She began to cover the displaced stones sweeping the soil and autumnal debris with a rosemary branch, releasing a fragrance that far from pleasing her, worried her brow. She stooped further within her world.

"There are more painful stings than those of a Mediterranean scorpion, Ana. The sting of war damages the memory irrevocably."

"Memories can be put away Tita; stored where they don't interfere with daily living."

"Not for long dear. Sometimes a face, others a voice or a certain scent brings memories tumbling down, lacerating wounds that never heal. I have never since planted, nor cooked with rosemary without hurting."

"Since what, when? "

"Since then. You see… mother cooked us the last meal we

Ana and her messenger birds

had in Guernica with rosemary. She boiled "Pepa" , our laying hen, for hours, adding chickpeas and all sorts of edible wild greens to the broth, until the hen's old age was macerated under the watchful gaze of our hungry eyes, coveting her loyal bones. That last meal perfumed the empty rooms and left the rosemary scent lingering in the whitewash of the walls and the memory.

All morning and the day before we had been selling and exchanging our meagre household belongings, between the neighbours who were staying behind and those who were travelling in different directions. There had been a constant hustle and bustle in and out of the home, with transactions being agreed in whispers over the kitchen table, until this was also sold.

When Monday morning came, our home was an empty shell and like it, it produced strange disconcerting echoes, which had us, children, very quiet for fear of disturbing the new spirit inhabiting the white expanse of walls. Only the rosemary scent remained and was left behind, clinging to the whitewash and wooden frames, to remind us of the safety of our lost home life. Two generations of mementoes and our future dowry kept in three camphorated chests had been badly sold, pawned or exchanged for travelling goods, while my sisters and I chased ghostly echoes around the emptying rooms of the house. The adult reality with its sacrifices and crimes was a remote world to us, a dogma we children had to believe in without ever seeing it, mother assured us, and to that effect, father had had a brilliant plan. Ours was a holiday, a long trip to Valencia where the Republican government was relocating to, for the duration of the civil war, and father…he would join us there, mother explained, fastening our travelling bundles to our backs.

The door was finally closed and bolted with parsimony, with only a few seconds in which to look back, for us to retain the image and print it with the indelible ink of children's memory, so we may never forget, my mother said. Though innocent and shielded from the awful truths that affected our world, we knew it to be the last glance at our door, our home, our street and town and all familiar things, in the lingering farewells between mother and the neighbours, in the silence of those good-byes and in the tremor of the ground under our feet with each new explosion over the surrounding hills. We knew it in mother's countenance and we knew it in our hearts when she turned the old ornate key twice within the rarely used lock, sending ripples of metallic sound waves through the bare passages and rooms that reverberated in our ears like a death sentence. She hid the key in her undergarments, where she had sewn all the money and documents for safekeeping.

We walked in silence, laden with our possessions, mother holding Rosa, your mother's hand and Ana, your namesake, holding mine but other groups joined our sorry party, absorbing us in their march towards the main streets, and there we were swallowed up by the human traffic, a mournful tide moving south, a wave of families, neighbours, retreating soldiers, old and young carrying heavy loads or just themselves but all inevitably looking around, to catch a last glimpse of the street and shops and landmarks, and acquaintances making unnecessary purchases in the street market. Because it was a Monday and market day, traders were cashing in on the buying and selling fever. There were even farmers offering beasts to the fleeing population, "at ridiculous prices" they shouted amongst the multitude to make themselves heard.

The crossing of the town lasted an eternity through the main arteries; these being busier than on procession days, for which we were caught in the stampede when the bells of all the churches began tolling for danger, and the marching multitude scampered in all directions, in a panic, with the natural centrifugal force that urban bombing has on the frightened population. Most took to the fields putting distance between their lives and aerial landmarks, and many others took refuge in churches and other sturdy public buildings, while those carrying large burdens, hung onto their belongings under prominent eaves and porches. Mother rushed us to the town orchards and there, under the apple and carob trees, we found shelter like dozens of other small groups did.

From our position under a carob tree, we saw that single bomber dropping his entire load in the centre of Guernica…and we bided our time for the second plane, and for the rest.

As the bulk of the people in the orchard were children and women, prudence and patience were observed. We were told and helped to climb up the trees, to perch on the sprawling branches, while the older women stood up against the tree trunks, waiting, coveting the unripe carob beans that hung in bunches of three or four but only children were allowed to eat. And that second bomber still to come...

Contrary to our privileged position, in the barley and cornfields north of the road into Guernica, the aerial cover was minimal. The desire to put distance between life and death drove most of our neighbours to the open road, forming a caravan of all sorts, badly protected by a handful of soldiers of mixed ideology. And that second bomber still to come...

Mother told us to scan the sky from the higher branches, but from our lookout it was easier to observe the fateful exodus of our neighbours, than to spy the immense blue. The caravan progressed slowly, noisily, laden with crying babies and children, and quiet mothers and fathers, and old people, and overloaded asses and mules, and hurried sheep and cows, while we waited under cover for some time, counting the friends we saw marching, forgetting that bomber still to come, repeating their names to remember those we might never see again.

No sooner had the caravan began to thin out towards Bilbao, a squadron (of the Condor Legion we learnt much later) aligned its Junkers over it, in descent and began to fire-bomb all their way to Guernica, littering the road with holes and bodies and blood and laments. A tangle of limbs staining the concrete and the broken hedges. Burst suitcases had strewn personal contents that flew over the dead, and landed in puddles of blood, and frolicked with the breeze to rest all over the surrounding corn. Bloodied photographs and bloody death spread by an unknown enemy.

Ana and her messenger birds

Oh Ana, we had no quarrel with the German people!! They had no reason to pound the entire town for two and a half hours until the evening glowed ablaze and the contours of its geography tumbled down, nothing but holes, like the leftovers of an abused Gruyere cheese.

During our exodus, we heard disturbing tales about the fate of our town and neighbours but mother's determination to take us to Valencia never wavered, bent on meeting father there. There wasn't any time in her schedule to stop and regret, to dwell on our losses, to mourn our Ana. She died, our sister Ana died, your namesake…she died in a hurry and in that instant her name ceased to be pronounced, until you were born Ana."

"But Tita, don't you know that granddad was already dead, that the meeting in Valencia was a ploy to keep you all afloat?"

But Tita could not hear my version of events. It is difficult to change the memories of the dead. All the same, she continued her narrative unburdening her heart.

"But that dark day in history had a darker night in our memories Ana". Tita Celia ventured in a flat voice and continued in a whisper. " We had approached the river in the twilight of the burning landscape, crossing orchards and meadows under a consuming spirit to reach the safest crossing point, and the further we were from our town, the darker the evening grew, and the more luminous were the flames on the horizon.

We were grouped and regrouped by the river, amongst the vegetation, building a ghostly queue onto a stretch of water hardly used for its dangerous proximity to the rapids downstream. Some considerable planning must have taken place to organise the crossing because two unknown men appeared out of the night, to direct our undertaking and deliver us across, away from the carnage that would follow the defeat of Guernica.

We waited there for hours, bent on our haunches, huddled in big groups while still queuing. Adults prayed and children wet themselves in fear. At midnight, one of the guides crossed the chest deep water tied to the rope that would be our bridge, secured at our end to the stump of an oak tree and was thrown a lasso in midstream by a young boy on the other side, directing the manoeuvre as if he knew the river bed, stone by stone: "your left foot forward. Now steady. Right one to the left. Stop and get used to the current. Left foot again..."

The guide reached the opposite shore, and the rope was tensioned and tied to another tree stump.

We still waited until the small hours for the myriad of fires over the horizon to dwindle, and then, in near darkness, and when our turn came, we began our fated crossing. Mother entered the river with Rosa, our youngest, your mother at her back and Ana, your namesake and oldest, followed her in with me at her back..." Tita Celia's voice quivered but she continued expiating her ghosts. " My sister Ana piggy-bagged me so we might withstand the mid-currents. Others had preceded us and many followed gripping the same rope in tense silence but... the waters ran cold and fast in mid-stream...and Ana was just thirteen...and her dress was heavy…and her foot slipped on the bedrock, where the rapids were but a hint in a carpet of slimy protuberances…and she lost her grip on the rope…and I was a heavy weight bearing her down.

By the token of our position, I stood higher over the water line and saw mother's hand outstretched, which I took holding Ana in a tight grip with my legs. We floated in that fashion for a few minutes, while mother tried to move us out of the current, but Ana ceased to struggle within the loop of my legs …and slid through my limbs like a fish unwilling to be taken from its liquid medium. And she went like a few others that opprobrious night; those few who were never found in the creek below the rapids, where we all camped until dawn, huddled in family groups.

Mother didn't utter a word that night and never again mentioned her name. There was never the right time to tell her that I didn't let her go, that Ana let go of me for some reason, that I loved her as much as she did…"

Tita Celia's narrative became a whisper, overcome by that grief of eternal measure which prevents my dead from resting. She tried to speak but uttered no sound, gesticulating what I could barely lip read as, "We tried so hard, so very hard to forget when oblivion is death itself" but, I could not guess whether she was communicating with me, her sisters or talking to herself. This said, she stood up and departed leaving the back gate open.

I traced her footsteps through the meandering path that led to the beach below but my aunt was nowhere to be seen, vanished in a few seconds; only her rosemary scent prevailed… or it might have been that autumnal breeze…or perhaps the floating spray of waves spent against the pebbled shore. The weather was again closing in around the peninsula, with low heavy clouds darkening the day, though they held onto their liquid for some unknown reason. I quickened my pace back home, again forgetting to close my prodigious back gate, to find Ed in his chair and his solid reality amongst the ghosts of my garden.

We stared at each other breathing in agitated unison, when only one of us had been running and that air we shared was thick with summer perfumes. I approached his wheelchair taking a mental note of the floral changes around us, of his open ogling of my progress, my step, my gait, my eyes. I did not know how long Ed had been awake; whether he had seen my Aunt or if only my comings and goings had been visible…or more worryingly, there might have been nothing to observe but the tedious passing of time. But the bluebells under the pear tree were certainly there, and the climbers in full blossom were real and the scent of lilies could not be imagined.

I brushed his ear with my lips with the intimacy of a shared secret and whispered: " Didn't I tell you it could be done? Look at the fruit of my labour!"; though I knew stronger forces than my own had been at work to transform the parched savannah of my decaying garden and Ed's reserve. He let his eyes wander about us, to take in the myriad of changes achieved in a few hours.

" What are you digging in that corner, a pond? "

" I… I don't know yet, but time will tell, though in the

meantime the excavated soil can be used to top all the flower beds."

" You sound like a true gardener."

" I hope not! "

" Where did you learn such organic wisdom?"

" My Aunt Celia…" I answered, omitting the " Has just told me."

" Your aunt must have been a woman of resources"

" Yes, she had remarkable qualities. Her existence influenced and enhanced all those who were acquainted with her. When did you ever hear of a " manageress" in the dark decades of the Spanish dictatorship? And she did it. Until she died, she managed the shoe shop she entered as an apprentice in Baños, the town where Grandmother found her citadel if not the illusory Valencia. And she ran the manager's funeral and the shop so smoothly and efficiently, that nobody noticed the demise of its owner until one morning, six months later, a far removed cousin and heir from the neighbouring Valencia appeared on the doorstep, after the inspection of the town and its inhabitants had revealed the prospects of self-management too parochial for his city lifestyle, and he left young Celia in charge of his newly inherited emporium.

At the age of twenty one, and of a height towering over most men of her time, aunt Celia found the independence of single men and the economic strength to steer her life at will, as well as the pleasures of family life; since mother and I had moved in after father left us on my birth.

You know Ed, I was told that Tita agreed to receive us in the family home for economic reasons but, it was obvious from my earliest memories that sadder motives had moved her, though I never asked her for confirmation. I remember my mother's slow change from a wilful and unpredictable figure, from which I would recoil in fear during her choleric fits, turning into a penitent phantom, which noiselessly patrolled each room in constant prayer and self-hatred. She also took to dressing in mourning black and frequented the evening mass at San Antonio's with a piety she hardly felt for us at home. Cleansing became her motto. She cleaned and scrubbed the house from Monday to Saturday with penitent zeal, as she polished furniture, spring-cleaned cupboards every other day, and she ironed all-white linen, towels and underwear with daily assiduousness. So ferocious and continuous was her toil that the light travelling from the window to the table in the dining room glided with transparent emptiness, void of dust particles even in August.

Grandmother took the domestic developments ruminatively, cooking and baking and singing while doing it, invariably in good or bad weather, from dawn till dusk, when she would then tell me gruesome bedtime stories that sent shivers down my spine and she would cross her heart and kiss her right thumb to add veracity to them. I welcomed the change as a daily gift and got closer to my aunt, hungry for approval and tenderness. Tita Celia developed day by day, adapting to my mother's change, and to cover up her abandonment; one morning she started to dress me up before she went to work, on another evening she tucked me in at bedtime, some other time she kissed my forehead in grandma's presence, and one day I gave her a sonorous kiss while mother looked on in distaste, setting the pattern for a lifetime of maternal ambiguity for both of us.

Tita laboured to sustain our household like a dutiful husband. And in addition to it, she oversaw my education, tended to my physical needs and those of Grandmother, and even loved my mother when she would allow her to do so. Of all, she doted on me and the friends and neighbours I happened to take home for lunch. While we ate, as entertainment, she would read us articles from the papers and magazines at that tender age when children were taught " The sacred stories from the Old Testament to build the moral foundations so lacking nowadays", as my mother would say when passing by the closed door.

Mother's biblical presence, the outlandish culinary talents of Grandma and Tita's periodic lectures of headlines such as: " Man eaten by a crocodile in Nairobi" or " Miss Taylor married her fourth husband on Saturday " and " Two E.T.A. members crossed the Pyrenees on foot ", all contributed to that heady sensation of walking on the edge of a precipice during my childhood. Tita Celia would pace the dining room, not reading but declaiming those reports, while we listened in suspended animation and watched her gestures because she had an ornate face, of a topography difficult to capture in a photograph. Her facial expressions added meaning to her reading, her thick voice added more meaning to her meaning, that being just implied was perfectly inferred by a child. Her ambition was to let me know, to make me know. To show me all that was there to be seen, against all the odds.

During the long evenings of winter Tita would switch on

the radio to listen to the "Pirenaica", a political pirate radio station, sitting me by her side, and she taught me to sew, crochet and to embroider while we followed the world's news and programmes that the regime had censored. Grandma would sit with us and dozed until the music programmes began.

Sundays were intimate days, when mother would spend all morning in church affairs, grandma would bake for the larder, and Tita would invite me into her bedroom, to read to me (while still in pyjamas) passages from forbidden books of political or literary audacity like "The black spider of Blasco Ibáñez". I would climb inside her lavender scented bed and beg her for "one of those funny sounding books".

Then as she read beside me, my attention wandered about her sanctuary; my avid eye would measure and count the various perfume bottles and other porcelain pots and jars over the laced dressing table, to rest on the portable record player she bought in Valencia, which invariably had me asking her " Can I?" Her old favourites then filled the air with sultry rhythms of pasodobles, cha cha chas, and of Nat King Cole in Spanish. Those mornings the room shone with the romantic candour of the white linen and the overflowing lace, dressing the entire bedroom and balcony doors. The brightness of her private habitation was only blemished by her auburn hair spread over the pillow, which I frequently caressed and compared with my smaller version. She had no beauty like the heroines of her foreign books but there was a harmonious finish to her features and an exciting multiplicity of expressions in her elaborate face. Feelings and sensations exuded through her eyes and demeanour, to the delight of all that fell under her spell. Her spirit never succumbed to the shabbiness of that time and her direct stare never swerved under the regime.

Tita Celia belonged to no one, no man, no affiliation, no creed but Grandmother alone, since the beginning of time. She was as much known as Carolina's girl as Miss Celia. Her well carried spinsterhood quieted the men's rumblings over the domino tables outside the cafés, when they observed her walking to and from work:" There she goes...a crying shame...haven't seen a finer one." And children believed her to be a cross between an angel and a witch, somewhere astride between a playmate and a spare mother. And mother...to mother she was the cause of all her sins she would constantly say.

While Grandma loved her tacitly, with subdued adoration, well hidden behind her chocolate cake baking; in permanent fear of losing those she loved I understand now. Forever spying the sounds and the smell of the suspected death, of her imminent visit and pillage, while aunt Celia, who had been her second born, remained in second place in spite of all her sacrifices, never usurping a prayer or a thought bestowed upon the memory of Ana. This I realise now.

That's the purgatory my dead inhabit."

7 THE APPARITION

"What purgatory is that, Ana?"

Ed was puzzled. He had not been part and privy to my visitations and their disclosures and he could not guess the extent of their tragedy, when not even I was aware of it until yesterday.

"Do you remember the jewelled triptych? The third girl on it was my grandmother's oldest. Ana as she was called, died the night of the bombing of Guernica...drowned in the river. Grandma could only save one of her daughters...while the other drifted away..."and so, I told him the tragedy in detail.

"And you think that your grandmother and your aunt never came to terms with the death of Ana?"

"I think they both believe they let Ana die while they survived...to regret it."

"Didn't they ever talk about it?"

"There was a tacit agreement to erase memories of the war years, to avoid reprisals at the hands of the victors and to avoid the ultimate revolt by those vanquished. That symbiotic alliance of mutual fear and economic dependence between the people and the regime had created a vacuum between "our glorious distant past and brilliant future"; in which the dead rested unclaimed, the missing were not searched for, and the living turned deaf and dumb in that parable that was our present out of joint, and all... to avoid a second Armageddon, brother killing brother, neighbour raping neighbour. But base and pure passions simmered together beneath the civility of the dictatorship years.

Now Ed, I guess their endeavours have come to nothing, encumbered with guilt in death as when they were alive, my relatives still wander without course...in their purgatory."

"You can't know that for sure, Ana. Perhaps all their memories died with them. "

"I'm part of their memory as much as they are mine. Don't you see? Their individual differences are my family traits, their reactions to their tragedies were my upbringing, grandma cooked the dishes you eat today by my hand."

"That may be your inheritance not their eternity Ana. It would be monstrous when I die, shortly, to hover in that abyss missing you eternally or regretting my unrequited love for you, no, I hope to find pe..." But he had said too much.

"Would you rest in peace were I to mourn you until my days were over?" Oh, I resented his love, my affection, our predicament, my outburst, and I resented my resentment!

"That's cruel my beloved Ana. Unrequited love is an absurd bittersweet torment but if having you near in my last hour has to be a platonic affair, so be it; I even enjoy the displeasure of my desire...and that of my recent inadequacy...mind you, I wouldn't acquiesce with my circumstances so easily, were I to wander in death fettered to your memory for ever, loving you as today."

"Stop, stop it! You are torturing me!

I knelt on the footrest of his wheelchair and held him by his shoulders and made him look straight into my eyes." What do you want from me?"

"I don't want to get what I most desire. I fear my sickness, your derision. I…can't perform for you my Ana!" He cried in desperation, sobbing each wet word," But I need you, I need your glances, your presence, your life!"

"You shall have me then, every bit of me that can be given," I said, sealing my covenant with a kiss of life and death. Our only means to find his peace…and mine. We held the embrace for a while, reluctant to separate in two broken halves, his buried in the nape of my neck, mine staring at the darkening skies summoning all my strength for the days and months to come, missing him already.

"Will you ever forgive me for what I have forced you into Ana?"

"We can't force feelings into existence Ed. Affections are born without invitation, without consent, without a name until we give them one. On my part, I can't swim any longer against a tide of emotions threatening to drown me. I will gladly bear a heartbreak tomorrow if it was worth it today. Let this be our motto."

His warm eyes pierced the depths of mine with new impetus, drinking from the chalice, my thoughts, absorbing my new willingness, my newly named affection. I let him compromise my peace, to enable his own before dying. I had more days, months, probably years to live and find my peace.

Ana and her messenger birds

"My darling Ana, all my life I've waited for this moment. I chanced knocking at your door, a moribund after two years, to receive your precious gift. God has been generous to me!"

"Don't bring Him into it, here and now there is only you and me and much suffering in between!"

Time had travelled unseen across the three cardinal points of the peninsula. The sun was fleeing the oncoming eastern clouds with precipitation, while the breeze that the sunset stirred enveloped us, hissing again parts of that very old song of Silvio Rodríguez.

"Women offer here and there
Embraces to the men who dare..."

This time we both heard it and perceived the drop in temperature. Guessing what that might be the prelude of, I embraced Ed tightly, still in our position and whispered:

"Have you noticed?" " Yes," he murmured.

"Did you hear?" "Yes"

"There, as you are, look over my shoulder around the garden, but don't shout or move the wheelchair". To the uninitiated it was an odd request; however, he obliged sensing that something extraordinary was about to happen. " The garden Ana...looks splendid with spring and summer flowers! There's greenery everywhere and..."

"At the far corners, to the back?" I was leading my witness, anxiously gripping his back, dying of suspense in a suspended embrace now devoid of lust.

"What else do you see?"

"Those corners are still bare, lifeless. To the right beneath the hill-cut, the oleander you planted this morning has wilted under hordes of yellow scorpions crawling through its bare branches. In the left corner by the beach, that hole you excavated is flooded with murky water. The pile of soil by it is entirely covered by a blanket of moss spreading to the fence as well! "

Something else was about to happen, someone new bound to appear because the stage had moved on.

The atmosphere had deteriorated by some rising damp oozing from the depths of that pool. I could not move before it all began, afraid of spoiling the conjuring which had brought Ed into the magic circle wherein to witness the other life my deceased relatives appeared to endure.

"Is the gate open?" I directed his eye to the stage entrance.

"You left it open just now, remember? … Ana…I think you ought to see this, quick!" I felt his heart galloping against my body.

"Just tell me what you see Ed". In a whisper, for courage.

"There's an old woman dressed in mourning black standing against the setting sun that filters through the gate."

"That's Carolina, my grandmother," I interjected.

"Wasn't she twenty years dead?" Ed wondered.

"Yes." I confirmed nearly hearing the course of his thoughts and felt him gasp and miss a few heartbeats before resuming his impromptu narrative.

"She has turned her face to the beach and is calling someone there. Look!"

I could contain my curiosity no longer, kneeling on his footrest, lingering there within the crook of his body, seeing only the storm raging outside the perimeter of the garden. I turned and saw a diaphanous figure dressed in a white linen habit coming through that portentous gate, preceded by her elongated shadow.

She was of adolescent age, with angular features in my old familiar custom, her gait was familiar, as well as the colour of her hair, which flickered from chestnut to copper in the oblique dying light. She wore no shoes but instead of advancing clumsily over the unknown terrain, she glided toward my grandmother like a swan travels the waters, effortless and majestic.

Grandma took her hand, and both went to the digging works over the left corner.

"That girl must be Ana, the aunt I never met, my namesake." If Ed had seen the virgin, she would not have been so readily accepted, his rational mind would have rejected a religious apparition but this was not the personification of his beliefs, it was the memory of my dead relatives; and though I was better acquainted with the bizarre happenings in my garden, a prickly sensation watered my eyes because Ana could not be the projection of my memories, or my mind. The triptych was not mine but my visiting grandmother's.

"But…why? Ed groaned his puzzlement.

"I don't think they have found their place beyond their life."

"You knew this was about to happen, didn't you?" Ed reproached without anger.

I answered, skirting the truth, that, " I had never seen that scene before". Ed ruminated.

"If we aren't suffering a collective hallucination…"

"We are not, Ed, I had never seen that pendant triptych until Grandma left it behind two days ago."

He ruminated again. " They are … solid, as real as you and me…"

"As real as death… or God for some" was my suggestion to keep our feet on the ground but it backfired.

"His creation is a fact of his existence..." Ed proposed against all logic, but I, as ever, disliked the ease with which the existence of God is taken as a given. " Let's not lose contact with reality."

"There must be an explanation for what we are seeing here Ana."

" Is there a factual reason for your belief in God Ed?"

"Yes, me…well…no, I just do," he conceded flatly.

"And no questions asked? Without a reasonable doubt? Faith is a question of faith; belief in what you can't see but doubting what we are watching."

"But why is this happening, to us, to you, to me, now?"

"Why? And why not? Whatever the reasons we cannot turn our backs to it, you agree?"

"Please wheel me nearer that corner."

So, I did, meandering our way through the foliage that here and there competed for space and obstructed the paths at thigh level. There was a glossy newness on each and every leaf that basked under the furtive caress of that evening dusk, hyacinths inebriated the senses, fruit laden trees rocked their heavy branches by a breeze whistling through the open gate and gathering momentum at the far left corner. On our approach to the digging site, the breeze got colder, uncomfortable, circulating in flat whirlpools that dragged strands of gelid vapours emanating from the flooded hole around that wintry tableau. All natural noise ceased to follow our progress muffled by an intense cold. I suppressed a shiver, but Ed could not control the chattering of his teeth, sounding like a woodpecker in December. I had to leave him a few yards behind (well wrapped in his travelling blanket), while I fought the increasing chill gripping my bones and heart to reach the space where the twosome seemed to co-exist.

Behind me Ed was to observe what was to happen.

Grandma was digging her hole with tenacity. Her hurried diligence indicated a lack of time, some contradiction in her laborious eternity. She was thrusting her spade into the sodden verge of her pool with gusto, pushing it in with her left clog, pulling out the heavy load, thrashing it asunder and digging in again and again and again, while the girl toiled within the muddy water in the fashion of the rice planters I had seen in the flat Vegas of Valencia.

I took the other spade that was lying around whenever grandma visited my garden and joined in the digging, conscious of Ed behind us. It was not long before grandma acknowledged my presence in her usual cryptic manner. " Time is running out Ana". Or that was one of her deliberate riddles, or she was not yet aware of my presence.

"Whatever for grandma?"

"Poor, poor Ana! All those years completely alone, ambling in limbo, for what? How can there be any peace when a

82

mother can't find her lost daughter?"

"Oh, my daughter!" She lamented aloud.

"My daughter!" my mind cried in echo.

My thoughts strayed far, south to where my daughter Aurora inhabited a motherless world…having blissfully forgotten her painful orphanation twenty years ago. But I had not.

"What's Ana doing?" I asked her just to scramble images of my past reflected on the murky liquid, at my feet.

"Ana? She is just biding time until we all are at peace." I was at a loss whether she referred to me, or her daughter; her generalised statements could always be widely interpreted to suit all occasions, like old proverbs." Poor Ana!" She ceased her toiling, inhaled a lung-full of those gelid vapours and announced,

"There isn't much time left before night befalls us."

A dry frost was setting in on the soil, forming a volcanic surface of what had been the spoils of her digging, spread between moss patches and the coldness of their eternity, with the iridescence of freezing ice. Mist hovered over the improvised half-filled pond, it had reached my feet and was moving toward Ed's wheelchair and the back gate in a pincer movement…But the girl did not seem to notice, busy as she was planting innumerable seedlings in and around the ever-growing puddle, with oriental dexterity.

"What are you planting, Ana?" But it was grandma who answered for her." She can't hear or see you. She is only a reflection, the inhabitant of a pure world, painless, guiltless. Water attracts her for reasons she'll never guess."

Ana and her messenger birds

"That's fortunate, in her circumstances..." I offered tentatively.

"It certainly is, poor soul but in that merciful limbo, there are not beacons to illuminate the path, no coordinates where a thought might be sent, not a prayer or a malediction can taint her total peace...the anguish of those she loved will never disturb her rest...but your pool attracts her"

I thought of Tita Celia, searching the width and length of the universe, looking for her drowned sister."

I had voiced my thoughts inadvertently, trailing on where her voice had faltered when I felt the earth warming under my feet. Grandma was crying silent tears that rolled over her bosom to fall and mix with the rising mist, producing hot currents of liquid sorrow. The resulting mix engulfed them, and it would have swallowed me in its mournful depths had it not been for Ed's calling.

I turned to him barely discernible in the darkness, then to the digging works but there was only a trace of mist sliding down the natural slope of the garden, through the gate onto the beach. Not the toiling figures of my grandmother and Ana.

A fine drizzle had started. The conjuring evaporated; without it the night emerged damp, cautious, formal. I wheeled Ed out of the cold drizzle, through the cold rain curtain to the conservatory. There we stood shaking and dripping, quietly, in an eloquent quietness where harsh rotund words would have distorted our understanding, where the unspoken took shape as tangible as Ed's faith.

8 A FREED SPIRIT

The house was cold. Uninhabited during a whole day spent in the garden, it had a monastic air in the lack of clutter that domestic use disseminates over available surfaces, exaggerated by the absence of cooking scents lingering in quiet corners, noticed in the sepulchral silence that the mantelpiece clock disturbed with its insidious tick-tock, and in the semi darkness of the unlit living rooms. I switched on all the lamps and lights on the ground floor.

In returning to life, our own, forgotten basic needs demanded satisfaction and had me running to and from the kitchen and dining room with food offerings, the medicine tray, and bouts of guilt for having forgotten his precarious health.

Now that most barriers had been lifted, that our two halves had formed a whole orange, the sweet and wholesome feeling of belonging had augmented the fear of the impending separation and the perspective of another loss tasted bitter indeed. Anxiety and hurt for my future hurt subdued my demeanour and Ed felt it.

"Come on Ana, sit near me and let us have this supper before the night dissolves away", he said tapping the chair on his left." I'm well taken care of. My aches are no one's fault."

Idid so, locking in all my apprehensions and we shared the pâté sandwiches, salad, fruit and chocolate. It was a treat to share his good company (it had always been) and to forgo the austerity of the solo eater, and to savour the pleasure of eating and romancing over the tablecloth. The food spread was an inviting banquet. Ed still cut a fine figure. The toasted slices of French bread smelled of intimacy. It had been so long since…

"You are blushing Ana", Ed teased, blandly aware of the shortcomings of our relationship, but I found a safer ground for table conversation. " What do you think my grandma meant by, there is not much time left before time befalls us?"

His flippancy dissolved, his expression sobered, his rational mind at work and dangerous intimate teasing was abandoned.

"I'm not insane, I wasn't yesterday, so the chance of being so today is remote. And they were as real as you were there conversing with them; my beliefs unfortunately do not provide for all contingents. We must reason this through, free pathways and unlock memories buried deep within you under secret codes. Why do you think I came back to England Ana?"

"To find peace near me?"

"Before it might have been too late, before the night befell me, but your grandmother could not have meant my impending end because her memories were never part of mine or vice-versa. Her cryptic message belongs to you Ana."

"But I have no recollection of the events I have been told recently by them. They all seemed to have lived secret lives within the same roof, in which I wasn't included; perhaps to protect, to shelter my innocence…"

"Or to bury their collective guilt. They obviously sympathise with your failed attempts to bury your past, so either they want you to help them or they want to help you."

"We are assuming that they are real, but they aren't physically so. How can I cross the gap that divides our different solidities, without dying first?"

"What if you let them make the first move?"

"I lost my daughter Aurora that way…" There it was. I said it. I had candidly fallen in his tender trap (or was it my own?) and I was ready to offer the contents of my box of secrets, while Ed held my hand over the table encouraging confidence with his ever contagious smile.

"What happened in your marriage Ana?"

"There was not a marriage…I mean there was but only in name. It was a brief farce staged and managed by my then husband."

"Brief farce?"

"Very brief; the time it took for his discharge papers to arrive at his lodgings, and a day."

"And a day," Ed echoed me, puzzled.

"An ex-gratia day in which his change of mind and heart did allegedly happen. During the three weeks that our marriage lasted and since Antonio went back to lodge with

Ana and her messenger birds

Doña Rosario while he found us a house, his daily visits had shrunk in duration and substance to a polite exchange of health and weather reports, and though that state of affairs didn't upset me, our uncertain future worried mother who saw her daughter growing bigger, and still living like any other single mother-to-be, a social pariah."

"I had seen him the day before, when he came blandishing the circular that made it official, but nothing was said about our future, nothing of it being separate affairs, and no plans whispered in tender tones. We were the most detached couple grandma had chaperoned in her time."

"But we were never lovers, a couple, a pair yes, married yes but we were not in love. We had lain together three times before I discovered my state, but since then, we were stranded between our different intentions, mine to delay the inevitable and his...well...I wasn't sure about his. I wasn't curious and he was never forthcoming with information but of one thing I felt sure during that last visit: he looked happy. His gait was relaxed, confident and his usually stern face seemed brighter than his regular ashen colour. He looked like a freed man."

The following day he took to Valencia, to make his fortune, he said. Of him I don't remember many physical details, as I have been always avoiding the smallest image, the slightest thought that may produce pain, but the impression he left in my memory is rooted like ivy to a tree, shaping my thoughts, restricting my way out of him....he feels like...drowning..."

"Try describing him to me Ana."

"I'm not sure I can."

"It will be alright."

"Can you promise?"

"No, but trust me, it's going to be alright", Ed said, pressing my hand.

"I can describe Antonio by what he isn't: He is not of average physique or mild temperament, not easy to escape his tentacles and he is not to be taken lightly."

"But you said you were married for only three weeks…"

"I met him (he met me) five years later, the night the General died, and our destinies have been one ever since."

"But he left you, didn't he?"

I could have said "yes" without hesitation but returning to that event and the impressions it left and feeling those impressions, I said: " I think we left each other. It appeared so because in those days I couldn't have made the first move and remained in town; though I chose to make the second one, to let him leave easily and refused to play the victim's game.

Just a note in the morning pushed under the door.

However, that very Saturday in the afternoon there was a knock at the door, easily confused with the police's calling card, disturbing the entire household and adjacent houses at either side. It brought us all to our feet; Grandma came out of her kitchen drying her hands in her black apron, mother sprang out of her room still clasping the Bible in her hand, Tita Celia and I rushed out of the living room, all converging in the spacious corridor which ran across the length of the house, from the patio to the double oak doors at the front and it had served as interior courtyard some many years ago.

Ana and her messenger birds

Tita opened the door after some hesitation. There against the pale Autumn sunlight, was my three weeks old husband, now in civilian clothes, flanked by two voluminous suitcases attached to his hands while he crossed the threshold and while he stood in the centre of the vestibule, erect, and cold as the northern wind. We all remained quietly expectant for different reasons, (not the homecoming of the returning husband), and before any of his in-laws formed a misleading impression of the visit; Antonio addressed mother, acknowledging me with an oblique sidelong glance, and a nod in my direction.

"You got what you wanted, Señora, and now it's my turn to get my freedom, as agreed."

"If I had what I wanted she wouldn't be carrying a bastard's bastard", mother spat her disgust for my predicament and her contempt for his intentions, pressing her Bible against her shrivelled bosom.

"All the same, I'm on my way up and set to find my long overdue prosperity in Valencia, alone, you know how things are."

Tita Celia held my hand behind my back in an implicit gesture of restraint, to let events take their course, to take a passive stand and let my mother be my mother. Grandma held a corner of her apron to her gasping lips, producing and smothering small cries. Mother stepped back to throw her voice as she cursed,"I will pray that you rot in hell. You sinful coward!"

"Now, now…Señora, I have made a decent woman of your daughter, at your request, so why don't you make a happy man of myself letting me part without acrimony."

"My daughter was a decent girl before she met you."

"I believe I leave her in good hands to continue being decent." He addressed us all as one entity, arresting his eye on my swollen tummy. Tita and I covered it with both our hands in an automatic gesture, presaging a danger sure to come by his hand...but, yet we did not foresee the gravity of things to come.

"I don't ever want to set eyes on you, degenerate you!" Mother proffered back- stepping once again, this time against the wall; to which, Antonio shrugged his shoulders, turned on his heels swinging the two suitcases around and made for the door. Grandma ran ahead of him to fully open the two doors, to speed up his exit and slammed them close behind him.

We stood there in the darkened vestibule, rooted to the over polished stone floor, staring at each other's reaction, at the closed doors, and what had been left out of our domesticity, expecting a second knock, a change of heart, but after an interminable reflective minute it was understood that his departure from our lives was a definitive Adieu and nothing had been lost with it. There would not be tears shed over the loss of his acquaintance. Then I reached over to mother, who had turned to the wall to pray for forgiveness on all our behalves, and I pressed her frame with a conciliatory arm across her shaking shoulders, in an attempt to bridge the filial gap between us. All the years of neglect and disaffection meant but a skin-deep bruise to me if she had finally emerged from her hostile isolation and self-imposed martyrdom. My child, I thought, would bring enough love to spread around with generosity. My mother might learn to love her better than she had loved me, and her presence in our lives would make up for all her disappointments but…when mother felt my contact she shunned it, scurrying off to the kitchen muttering "You aren't better than him!".

Grandma straightened the coverlet over and around my body with kneading hands, after Tita had taken me to bed, and she busied herself brushing off the unruly strands of hair with her characteristic wrist movement, half caress half indolence, while grandma tucked me in and both fussed and spoke of the next day's plans and future ones to share with me and my baby daughter because: "I was carrying a girl" they prided themselves to know. All in aid of my motherless state. But I had never missed what I never had. I had always been my aunt's niece, liking what I saw in her eyes when she looked at me.

My two nurses left me to have a rest.

My eyes wandered around the room with the curiosity of a visitor. There had been one day in which a swift change had taken place within me and without. My attitudes and attachments had undergone a transformation in the claustrophobic lapse of twenty-four hours. Yesterday, as many days before the wedding, I had paused by the mirror to call myself my husband's wife, and invariably I had felt vertigo, the repellent attraction of an approaching precipice, pushed by my own hand, and I had wanted to stop the fall.

Yesterday Antonio had wanted to be a freed spirit, and the day he left I was one too, and that sense had sharpened all the others, increasing the intensity of colours, shapes, sounds, smells and of life itself.

The heavily varnished oak furniture, the fitted bookshelves, the whitewash of the uneven walls, the windowsill dressed in ruby coloured geraniums, they all beckoned my return to the family fold. I had been at the brink of a precipice and turned around in time and found my safe haven as I left it before I lost my innocence; though it would not be safe forever I discovered some years later.

I took stock of my possessions and began to arrange my future:

I would continue my English studies.

I would take that receptionist post in the Languages Institute.

I would earn mine and my daughter's keep.

I would take her to Valencia on holidays.

I would help Tita to manage our home.

I would be the mother I never had.

I would learn to bake Grandma's chocolate cakes…

…and the list of musts and don'ts kept growing, filling my future with a solid purpose, a centripetal force around my baby, my daughter, that familiar structure of my odd family arrangement without a single man in it, what good and not so good that existed in the reduced circle of our home, those shades of me unbeknown to all but Tita. Me. My aunt's niece, my mother's shame, my Nana's culinary receptacle, an abandoned wife with all its advantages, a freed spirit. The odds were not so odd as to impede a reasonable life under the regime, as long as I kept a low social and political profile, like most of us then .

The bittersweet aroma of baking chocolate began to ascend from the kitchen and filtered through the thick walls and doors. The neighbours had often said that they could smell grandma's chocolate cake baking. Tita often said that the street knew of our troubles for the cooking aromas that followed them. Mother always warned us of the punishments for gluttony. I felt a sudden urge to eat a few portions of Nana's miraculous remedy for all ailments; it had been filling forever the holes created by the estrangement left by my devout mother.

I followed the aroma downstairs, bypassing the ever-busy figure of my mother, armed with bucket, water and Vim powder, scrubbing the flagstones in the missionary position; her Bible close by on a chair (just in case). The vestibule shone under a dustless light, like the immaculate but eroded interior of a convent. But mother was not deterred by the progressive thinning of the floor, which during her countless cleansing bouts over twenty years had lost half of its original thickness, being those days a step lower than the rest of the house. It was her way of erasing an unwanted presence: the memory of my ephemeral spouse... or that of hers; which obstinate like herself, still lingered around the red geraniums of Tita Celia, and every so often I would hear her saying about them, " those impudent plants shout the crimes of your father".

Unlike her, I had no morbid penchant for tragedy and melancholy, and did not harbour a broken heart. On the contrary, I had already forgotten the scent of Antonio, obliterated by the perfume of furniture wax and floor cleaning liquids…and those baking aromas escaping the kitchen in an edible mist had started to cloud the mirror by the front doors, making it cry with anticipation. I could not resist any longer.

In the kitchen, Grandma laboured feverishly with cake ingredients and baking gadgetry to make a second cake, having the first one cooling on the windowsill. One would have thought of baking two cakes from the start, on principle and in view of the persistent demand and shortage, but not her. Her second was always an afterthought, a token should it happen as usual that the first cake might not be enough. Her second cake making had maintained her limbs nimble and her matriarchal status unchallenged.

Like a one-man-band, her movements were fast and precise; not one idle crossing from the sink to the stove, from the pantry to the kitchen bench. One hand opened the cocoa tin while the other used to beat the eggs and another switched the express cafeteria off, while the other hand tasted the meringue mixture to verify "the snow point", and her eye checked the rising sponge in the oven, while her mind calculated the overflow limit of the pots soaking under the dripping tap. I spied the scene for a moment leaning against the doorframe, not daring to disturb those tender hands and their industry. Her marzipan shape, perennially dressed in black layers of mourning, underskirt, skirt, apron, vest, blouse and shawl, beckoned me to the table with a nod. The night had descended furtively from the ruined castle at the top of the hill where the town rested, to cool down the first cake. There were a number of passers-by on their way home, who lingered by the window to praise the cooling cake and who, when exclaiming " Not another one of your cakes Carolina!", they would receive a portion to eat on their way. I sat to eat my portion, still steaming as usual, warm and moist inside and crispy on top from the soda. Grandma observed my eating under the sickly yellowing of the naked light bulb suspended in mid-air, listening to my pleasure with eagerness; her right eyebrow quizzically arched while registering every gesture and guttural noise of my delight; tradition closely followed since that recipe was concocted by her foremothers. I in turn inhaled, moaned and rolled my eyes in ecstasy so she could relax and join me.

We were not gluttons and the pleasure was not just in the eating of that cake, it was in the bitter-sweet taste of the extravaganza in bad times, it was in the aromatic warmth that its baking created, also in the ceremony of cutting and sharing which bonded the eaters, and it was in the awakening of all senses, as the portion was consumed, producing an inflated sense of wellbeing.

The clacking of heels up and down the hill, that reverberated in the kitchen, were discernible as to their gender and direction. The creaking of furniture became audible like old bones in old bodies. The scent of Grandma's labour thickened across the table. Dangerous thoughts had their wrinkles ironed into velvety, chocolate texture.

Grandma mumbled as if perchance: " To a fleeing foe, offer feathers far afield", digging her fork in her portion with incisive force to separate a bite. I waited for clarification, but her proverbial wisdom often travelled incognito, open to mystifying interpretations. That was the strength of her good company, that versatile attitude for conversation, never mindless but often rhetorical, lyrical when left to wander in monologues, prosaic and utilitarian when passing biased verdicts, and proverbial to create atmosphere, to show veracity.

She cut me another slice of the misty cake and chuckled while handing it over to me, " have your cake...and eat it"...and that remark was a drop too many, the uncorking of our composure that brought a flood of mixed feelings to the surface in hysterical laughter. And laugh we did, to our hearts' content.

We laughed at my mock marriage. We laughed at his desertion and laughed because his child would be ours to keep and we laughed because our home would never house a man. And we laughed because, crying, one does it alone.

Mother came in to empty her bucket in the scullery, scaring away our mirth and the aromatic mists.

"Gluttony is another of your sins!" She threw her spite into the sink with the dirty water, frightening the pots and pans with her tirade riveted with passages from the "apocalypse."

I felt grateful that her malady had flourished within the confines of religious fervour and not in the political arena or the carnal pleasures; thus we let her do and say what she saw fit and continued our eating when she calmed down.

Aunt Celia came home from the afternoon shift she had to cover for a few hours. We were on our third slice of chocolate cake, and she joined us at the table as usual, full of anecdotes from the shoe shop: " There had been a man who we knew well enough, of mild temperament and homely virtues, who had bought a pair of platform shoes size four; when his lady wife (Tita forwarded) was a generous six. And there had been a quiet woman we knew better still, who had brought back (before closing time) the very same pair of size four and between blushes and apologies demanded a refund in cash."

Life was seldom boring, days hardly predictable where life and death happened under the unnatural bent of religious dogma and political oppression. The General had imposed so many limitations in the country that it was impossible to spend a day without breaking a rule or two.

Tita Celia related this and other spicy comings and goings in the shop. By then the memory of Antonio had receded to the outskirts of town; the vestibule had never received such a visitor, the living room could not remember him asking me to marry him, even his name had shrunk to Toni…and my bedroom would never cease to be mine.

And no, we were not callous women, as it might appear, but we had an innate instinct to survive when we had a reason to do so. My daughter. And for it I relied on my Aunt, she on Nana and Nana in turn relied on her infinite wisdom from past experiences going back to her own grandmother's and (that failing), she trusted the close relationship between mother and God on the assumption that God might be sympathetic to those so devoted to Him, because if one of us were to falter, our supporting house of cards would disintegrate to the demise of all of us.

Ana and her messenger birds

We were aware of the lack of men in our family; however, ours was a minor ailment to which mutual care was the right medicine, while many other families feared worse. There was a pathological phobia in the country to hear that knock on the door preceding the arrests or disappearances of those male relatives we did not have. Sometimes men "who helped the Guardia Civil with their inquiries", suffered minor accidents on their way back to their homes, or at best, continuous unemployment would drive him and his family out of town as local exiles.

In the cases where a family had been left fatherless, mothers and daughters depended on their relatives or charity, because women were not taught a trade as breadwinners. The charity offered to all and sundry depended on the church, while the church's power lay in the hands of the General, and his supremacy fed off the fear and poverty of my defeated people, who toiled to merely survive…and thanked the Lord for his provision through the church and its charitable work.

We, of course, had been spared those hazards in our amazonian household, and we were grateful to life, that in all her pettiness had given us an advantage; except mother who was only grateful to God for having given her only one daughter to despise.

So, with resilient hopefulness we savoured the second cake until well into the night, perfectly certain that tomorrow always came, bringing another day with it. The day came, and that day lasted five years,
and then,
my night descended.

9 A DEADLY EXCURSION

Ed had been born under a temperate democracy and found it difficult to comprehend certain aberrations of conduct by which animals and oppressed people learn to survive and thrive in a hostile environment. The more he gasped in shock the guiltier I felt for having disrupted his world, for disturbing the image he had of me, but it was too late to remain distant and mysterious. We did not have enough time for poise and subterfuge. My mistakes, my hurt and me were one indivisible entity; a Trinity that needed to be understood.

He wanted to know why he loved me.

I too wanted to know why he loved me because no man had ever loved me. My very first mistake in life, like the original sin of Eve, closed to me the doors of paradise, the Eden of happy families and multiple births, and it had set in motion a chain of events that culminated in my nomadic existence.

"Didn't your husband try to see his daughter?"

"Not through me or any of us."

"Didn't you think of him…wonder whether…"

Ana and her messenger birds

"It's all too easy to judge with hindsight but unfair."

"I wasn't my dear Ana; merely unfamiliar with the Spain of Franco and also curious about the reasons why my storyteller condenses five years in one sentence." Ed seemed eager.

"Are you interested in history with a small "h"?" I procrastinated.

"The facts experienced by the individual I believe…"

"The small lives and happenings of a town? " (I was reluctant).

"The questionable source of memories, legends, matrons and historians," Ed went on undeterred.

"The scent of ancestral memories linger about our bodies, but it is not very reliable," I replied.

"Ah! The fragrance of a woman's reticence," he toyed.

"Well then, I shall sprinkle you with some of my perfume," I announced, for I was ready to make more concessions … and he felt it.

Abandoning his jocular affectation Ed asked, " Were those five years happy ones?"

I finally relented to the opening of another wound. I had squandered my past with neglect, but the opprobrious memories had not vanished…nor had the pain improved with age. It still hurts to think of things. Faces were fading but deeds remained clear …Dates were hard to come by…

"It's difficult to summon the past at will, when I am used to hiding it from myself but there are certain memories that spring out of familiar smells, to catch me unawares, then a gesture…a glimpse and my macabre Jack- in- the- box pops out when least expected. Of all, the heady scent of petrol has the worst effect on me. The remembrance it brings hasn't yet diminished with time. Not only does it echo the death of half of my family, but also marks the origins of the disintegration of my small world, my reality, my then assiduous certainty…

That smell…those fumes!

The cries and pleas of the dying cargo inside that bus…that precious cargo that was consumed by the flames.

Tita Celia, my baby daughter and I had boarded the second bus, while mother and Grandma took the front seats still available in the first one. Mother was very fussy about close spaces and travelling arrangements, for which she decided to board the first one, and Grandma went with her to keep her company. The two buses travelled within a hundred metres of each other, on an easy and quiet stretch of the road to the Valencian seaside north of the city. It was a routine Sunday excursion popular in the early seventies, with scheduled stops across the mountains, valleys and villages stretching the whole width of the province, toward the flat land of the capital, all three landscapes in constant succession, and eastbound. The road meandered amidst grey, silver and violet tones under the rising sun. The endless orange and olive groves, and some carob trees in between at either side, had not yet regained their true colours. The continuous skirting of hills on the right had us travelling with the sun behind and facing us alternatively, in zigzagging fashion, now the first bus disappeared from view, now we caught up with it before the next bend.

On one of those blind bends, fate overtook us.

Ana and her messenger birds

We lost sight of it. There was a tremor...or a thunder...or both, whose force jerked our vehicle and shook the oranges off their trees. The driver made an emergency stop, throwing us off our seats and leaving us in no doubt of the seriousness of what might lay ahead. I threw my baby daughter into my seating companion's lap and began to press and push my way out, with Tita Celia and the more agile women travellers.

Outside, the smell of petrol was nauseating, and our violet dawn was turning orange. A black column of thick smoke sprang out of the hill before us, rising above the trees like a twister. We turned the bend in a frenzied race, saw the bus in flames and still ran towards it in thoughtless desperation, like a stampeding herd until the heat from the flames barred our way.

My mind tried to run, it ordered me to ...

...but my body did not enter the fire.

By my side and behind me other women attempted it as they remained welded to the ground while all arms gasped for entry to rescue those inside whose cries were audible over our own. Our driver had gone into the flames. His legs carried him who had no relatives burning ...and I and my Aunt still remained there on safe ground with the others, on all fours like a pack of rabid dogs."

"What happened to the driver?"

"He burned alive."

"...And to your mother and grandmother...?"

"They too...Tita and I lost half of our family in what was suspected as a terrorist attack, killing civilians, by some ETA splinter group, who thought that attacking the regime was not enough to achieve their aims after the imminent death of the dictator.

Our tragedy affected Tita Celia in unthinkable ways, she sank within herself, gravitating about the house in a somnambulist trance while I ...well, my breasts dried up by the shock ...or might have been that my mourning body could not supply my existence with tears and milk at the same time, as I could never feed two opposing sentiments with just one heart.

It was a sorry sight of my maternal drought that brought my Aunt back from her isolation; however, a new dimension had been added to her well-defined character. Small traces of Grandma had been imprinted on the periphery of her speech since the funeral and a tendency to melancholy had slightly clouded her perennial Sunday's mood.

Otherwise Tita Celia remained intact.

She still had her luminous strength born out of some mysterious gift to find joy in minute sources and "the mission she had in life to see me happy", she used to say to all and sundry. She reckoned that my milk might have been "poisoned with the tragedy and all that", but that "It was better that way". "Every cloud has a silver lining"; she grew fond of saying.

On the seventh day of mourning Tita opened Grandma's well stocked larder and began, from then on, to produce such aromatic chocolate cakes, that the sensuous purring of hungry cats could be heard again by the kitchen window, and the sound of sniffs and sighs of a shadow in the scullery became a feature of her cooking sounds.

We did not know how it happened, whether the layout of the kitchen helped to preserve the cooking secrets or that she had been unaware of the learning process through years of observation, whether it was hereditary or a nurturing need that drove Tita to the culinary counselling perfected by her mother. Whatever caused that distinct domestic change, it made life bearable. It lent a veneer of normality to our daily chores once performed by both our mothers to perfection.

Tita tried to prolong the pretence for mine and my daughter Aurora's sake. She kept their rooms cleaned and aired, in waiting. All past tenses disappeared from her conversations when these involved our mothers as if they were on some long-haul holiday and due to come back at any time.

But bit by bit the dust began to gather around us.

Tita Celia started to lose the thread of routine conversations. She had lost more than a mother and sister, they were (I know now) her past, they were witness to her exodus from their native Guernica in the Basque region and the reason for her spinsterhood. From then on Tita alone held the family memories, having to reconcile her agony with the knowledge that the perpetrators were also Basque, though I was not aware of it then.

And the inevitable happened one afternoon that winter, while we were lighting up the fire in the sitting room, busily sorting out the kindling wood, kneeling by the old hearth, when Aurora articulated her first words, " Tita Nanaa! look", pointing at Tita's hair and trotting drunkenly into her lap grabbed her hair shouting " Nanaa!". It was then when we noticed that Tita's mane had turned from auburn into a cascade of silvery white curls. It had been a spontaneous and sudden change. Her pride, and most valuable asset, was the only visible sign of her desolation; nonetheless she managed a smile and mimicking Nana's utilitarian philosophy she added " Better this than the Bible, don't you agree with me?"

10 THE SECRETS OF A SUITCASE

I have tried so hard Ed, to quiet my senses, to subdue memories, to put distance between my demons and myself but all has been in vain. Since that remarkable transformation by the fireplace, I associate that particular aroma of hot bricks that emanate through warmed roofs permeating the streets when all chimneys are working with my dear aunt, during her last winter.

It was an unusually cold November. All around us, and where there were enough means in the south side of town, the vapours of brick, tar and wood reacting to the heat oozed and lingered in ghostly manes, levitating at ground level.

It had been a testing period, with long dragging evenings in our sparsely inhabited home, only lightened by the presence of Aurora. The kitchen had lain idle more often than not (though Tita tried in her spare time), and vagrant lint began to glide in the oblique winter light. The whole country had lain in waiting for so long, the "Generalísimo" was so old. We the people had been so patient.

Ana and her messenger birds

The gestation was at an end.

That day we took our home into our hands and left no recondite memory and piece of furniture where it had stood in yesteryears. The new arrangements fitted easier with the period of the building and its location in the hilly street, resulting in a nursery room for Aurora where Grandma had slept and a working room for two in my mother's sanctuary, both at ground level, with direct access to the patio. The miscellany of furniture accumulated through the years and purchased with no relation to each other was redistributed around. The dark Castillian pieces converged in the upper rooms, to be tempered by the virginal white linen and draperies dressing the bedrooms and frowzy lace from Toledo. The red exuberance of the pompon heads of my aunt's geraniums excused the severity of the heavy shapes in the furniture and brightened up the big expanse of whitewashed walls. The Colonial pieces of walnut fronts and curvilinear legs were gathered in the lounge and dining rooms, to disguise our defeat against the dust over the brighter colours. The nursery and working rooms were left to the bizarre collection of leftovers, arrayed solely to please the eye; no crucifixes hung above us anymore, no saints overlooked our sins but undraped French windows invited the mind to wander out into the Moorish courtyard. Tita Celia had devoted a good number of Sundays to it, since their arrival in town during the civil war. Our Alhambric refuge had been a stable and farmyard, like the other two at either side and three others back to back, forming an inner labyrinth of enclosed patios flanked by houses tightly erected by their original owners without a single rectangle. They seemed to have been planted...or stacked together like Sunday jobs, with much love but little talent, over the centuries and architectural fashions of each quarter but they had stood the passing of time and its wars, clinging precariously to the hillside. However, observed from the stork's sentinel post at the belfry of the northern church, that chaotic spread had a social purpose in perfect harmony with the town's life.

Like a spider's web, the maze of streets and alleyways attracted the village life to the central square, at the foot of the main church of "Nuestra Señora del Carmen" and, in return for the extreme centripetal power, the Square emanated the necessary social life, pumping material wealth and social purpose to the main arteries and interconnecting streets, maintaining a fine equilibrium.

This is the vision conjured up by the aroma of hot bricks but...

There are of course other scents.

Smells and aromas that remind me of the five years lapse between the last two nefarious visits of my husband. Morning dew drops over fresh vegetation... the musty scent of first rains onto dry soil... Nature and memories do not recognise frontiers Ed. I perceive sensations through the same senses I use for social contact and my past and present are inextricably fettered to quirks of nature. Nature speaks eloquently to the expectant nose, the attentive ear or that avid eye that searches for the familiar in the new and foreign, to find comfort in the reflection, and peace in the certainty of what once was but is no more.

Many a time that drying washing, hanging on the line by mere pegs flapping to and fro at noon, exudes a scented praise for the forgotten labour of my mother, echoing of old Sundays' cleanliness with visions of her industrious red hands and the innocence of the white linen years.

Toni, my estranged husband, is a comma and a full stop at either side of my five year's paragraph, breve marks written in indelible ink.

That is the reason why, when Toni reappeared on our doorstep that very day of changes, after five years of absence, the day the General was about to die, we mistook him for a neighbour in need. Because he was the last person we expected to see that crucial night at that late hour, as much as I reckon I might have been the first name he must have uttered when he saw his political demise approaching that November in 1975.

Because the coming death of the dictator prompted our reencounter and his following visit brought about my exodus, my first husband is sadly linked to my past, present and uncertain future. His role in my life, though shortly played, darkened the radiance of my country's coming of age.

That night, the night that Franco was going to die, Tita Celia went to close the curtains in the upper rooms while I did likewise downstairs; this time re-enacting the fortification ritual for real. We had barricaded ourselves many times before, when there were rumours of searches after political unrest or a bomb explosion. Tita Celia would spring into action giving the orders for the drill while I... obeyed unawares of the true reason, admiring her dedication to detail, never suspecting that we might have been suspects in the town's list of undesirables because I never knew we were also Basques as were the E.T.A. terrorists.

That night Aurora had gone to bed unusually early after the excitement of a day of changes resulting in a new playroom. The house stood silent but for the radio transmitter in the sitting room, reciting in neutral tones the last hours of the "Generalísimo", extolling his character and recent achievements in a monotone pattern, as if the life of the news reader depended on his detachment from that crucial bulletin. We felt that this was to be the night because all radio programmes were periodically interrupted to report Franco's deteriorating health in minute detail.

We locked ourselves in. I changed station for corroboration and another monotonous disaffected eulogy was spreading the same coded message: Franco was about to die.

The future of our nation was to come at last!!

Spain did not sleep that night. Tita and I sat our vigil in the kitchen. She sat rigidly with her back tensed and straight, pale, immobile, deep in thought, fidgeting with her rings and toying with the monumental house keys resting in her lap, for a long time, until her voice broke out of the depths of her memories to prophesise: " That cruel little man shall never find his peace... like father...like your mother and mine...like Ana!" She said like a rabid dog. "Ana" I took it to be me then, but I know now that it was her sister.

"We should let sleeping dogs lie Tita or we will cause a second carnage bigger than the first,"

Ana and her messenger birds

"The sleeping dogs lie scattered about school grounds, nunneries, mass graves," she said with her voice as dark as the November night. There was nothing I could say to mitigate pain I did not fully understand at the time, for I did ignore the enormity of her loss and the circumstances.

We were at a loss in the new reality; she was mourning all the wasted lives and deaths across the decades, I feared the future, thus time oscillated in painful suspension.

Then Tita began pacing the room like a caged animal. I opted for the window and there I parted the curtains slightly but there was a dense blackness; no sign of life escaped from the doors and windows at either side of the street, the doorway lamps acting as street lighting were switched off, the moon was understandably absent. My spying post allowed me a diagonal view of the street downhill, which appeared to be a black hole of abysmal proportions. The entire neighbourhood had adopted a self-imposed curfew in fear of what may come after the death of the dictator.

The radio announcer exhausted his requiem and was closing the transmission with the details of the three-day's mourning period to come, in the event of Franco's death. When his voice ceased, my heart fluttered full of butterflies at the abstract prospect of freedom; there was the promise of the king in waiting...on the other hand, there was an army of people who having tasted the fruits of unrestrained power over thirty six years, might not be ready to relinquish it...on the other hand, there was a bigger army of Spaniards who having lived under the oppressors' yoke for three generations, had forgotten the original fear and had grown defiant... on the other hand, there was a lot to forgive and forget if we were to live in peace… but on the last hand, we had been indoctrinated by the Church to obey or suffer, to accept or be damned, to err and be punished.

There were so many hands to consider!

So many choices and opportunities to go forwards or backwards that the mere thought produced a dizziness of mixed euphoria and apprehension.

Tita Celia let a sigh escape her troubled bosom and whispered," The King …indeed…" and she reached for the lamp and switched it off, leaving us in the dark. By the window, the outside blackness gained life. I broadened the gap between the curtains and we observed with childish fascination how the night penetrated our secure observatory, spreading the same darkness within as without and gradually every shade of black became apparent between the shapes, surfaces and crevices in the down-rolling street; from where a lighter shade of black…more coal than pitch emerged, out of the night and up the deserted cobbles, dithering in its march.

Someone was lost at that bizarre hour of darkness before dawn.

We waited a bit longer. The approaching footsteps resounded hollow against the facades at either side of the street. Tita Celia reacted to that shadow impelled by past experience and fear whispering: "The door!", so we rushed to lower the archaic bar across it, but an imperative knock froze our movements. We looked at each other, not daring to utter a sound, while the caller persisted under the cover of total darkness. We swayed forwards and backwards, hesitated and pondered about the identity of our visitor also in the dark, hearing Grandma's voice saying " a night like this is plagued with dark deeds"; however the dictates of hospitality obliged and we opened the door still in complete darkness.

There stood a man squarely built to fill the entire opening of the right leaf of the double door, squeezed in a three-quarter length sheep's skin coat. He had two bulging suitcases resting on either side of his straddled legs. His face was a dark mass of obscured features.

"Are you lost, good man?" enquired Tita with forced optimism.

"Don't you remember me, Miss Celia?"

Ah! Sometimes the inflection in a word is more eloquent than an introduction, and that "Miss Celia" with insidious undertones had the effect of rooting us to the ground, it made all my blood plummet to the pit of my stomach and it dried Tita's throat.

"Well, aren't you letting me in on a night like this?"

My precious Aurora moaned in her sleep and Tita ran to the new nursery, to muffle the existence of his child before he remembered it. I was left to decide whether Toni came into our lives or went out for good. During five years Aurora had been " sweetie" or "the girl " or "your niece" but in that precise moment she became "my daughter" in the most possessive sense, when I remembered that the stranger facing me had also made a claim to her. An instinctive foreboding made me reach for the door handle to close him out of our lives, when an all too familiar sound of the army footwear of the "Guardia Civil" began at the top of the street.

Ana and her messenger birds

Cursed indecision!!

My estranged husband reacted to those boots by crossing the threshold with feline dexterity, suitcases and all, without disturbing the stillness of the night. When I closed the door he was already in, deep in the shadows of the corridor, and we stood still and mute in the dark recesses of the vestibule until the dreaded boots passed us by, leaving an ominous silence behind, replete with ears and eyes behind closed doors.

I could silhouette Antonio against the other familiar shapes around us, but I still remained quiet, unable to speak, observing him. It was not a physical impediment (it must be said) but the incapacity of being civil: I could not usher him in further in case my daughter became restless and noisy and I did not want to switch the light on and let him see my fear. I did not wish to see him, and so to remember him.

He took the initiative to show promptly that we were of one mind and that the occasion was not a social call. "I'm merely passing through, Ana."

I could not betray my fear and contempt. I knew my delicate position and his menace to our peace...and so did he. He dropped his luggage on the floor with a sonorous thumping.

"I'm sort of stranded...that is, I know where I'm going...out of the region if only I could get a taxi. All trains are station bound...there's nobody out to hitch a lift and my cases are too heavy. I could leave one suitcase behind in your care, to come back for it when the situation clears and walk to the nearest town through the quarry road, mind you... I could stay here until…"

Between his presence and his suitcase the choice was easy, though past knowledge of his behaviour told me that he did not gamble when the odds were even, for what I thought that he must have had a plan to get his own way…But I could not fathom what he was after, not in the state I was in; therefore I took a decision while there was a choice.

"I'll take care of your suitcase," I pronounced with a parched throat, opening the door to reinforce my meaning. He chose his right case and retraced his earlier footsteps to the doorway, stopping by me on his way for a second but neither of us spoke. Outside, he merged with the other dark shades of the upper street. I bolted the door and stood there against it paralysed in the darkness, regretting my choice for no apparent reason. I am not given to bouts of regret but somehow the interaction with my estranged husband did invariably make me count my blessings or regrets.

Oh, regrets and lamentations!
If we had bolted the door.
If we had not opened it.
If I had closed it when I recognised him.

We had been left with a suitcase that I was sure he had intended to leave with us. Tita came out of the nursery quietly asking, " Has he gone for good?"

"No, we have been left with this," said I, switching the light on to illuminate our temporary ward. It was a big rectangular brown suitcase, made secure by a series of ropes and knots, and locks to hold inside what was threatening to burst out of it. Its locks had been macerated to a pulp, and the broken zip was ornamental against bulging contents.

After two unsuccessful attempts to drag it on my own, I enlisted the help of my Aunt. We decided to store it upstairs, safe from prying eyes and out of our sight for what we understood to be an uncertain long time. Once at the foot of the stairs and by the weight of its contents, it became clear that we were not handling an ordinary load. Tita began pushing upwards from beneath while I pulled upward from four steps higher on the stairs.

"Isn't it too heavy for its size?" Tita mused as we hauled it a few steps.

"It's heavier than a corpse, this wretched thing," I huffed, and our eyes met across the same thought, though no word passed between us until we reached the middle landing. There we moved to one side and made room for our corpse to manoeuvre the corner. One of the ropes by which we were pulling it upwards gave way under the strain, and before we could restrain its gravitational force, it slid elegantly down like a comic piano, to burst open onto the vestibule, knocking on its wake the sentinel pot of geraniums at the base of the stairs.

Its contents were not our dreaded dismembered corpse, but hundreds of coloured folders, which on impact had spilled out their papered secrets, and lay on the flagstones in a confusion of pages, red petals and lumps of soil.

"What has that damned man brought us?"

"His dirty linen Tita," I muttered, glancing over some of the exposed dossiers. We began a hurried collection trying to match the insides with the folders by name, calling or identifying descriptions with photographs. Some were public personalities we recognised, others were strangers to us, and there were also a few town's people. To our knowledge some of those therein mentioned had since died or left town.

There was also detailed information of public dissidents: suspected sympathisers of this or that banned organisation, possible communists, atheists, anarchists, homosexuals and terrorists, in all, the entire pool of regional enemies of the state and faith were there, strewn like a fallen pack of cards.

"They must have everyone under surveillance!"

"We were not supposed to have seen this Tita please, let us put it away as it was," I begged.

"But …we can't! They are soiled and all mixed up. Toni is bound to notice Ana! Oh god Ernesto!"

My aunt aged a bit more around that agonising cry and sank on the floor holding a green file in her hands. She pressed it against her chest and picking some of the strewn geraniums in a distracted way she began rocking back and forth.

"He bought me my first geraniums for my twenty-third birthday," she said, and began to gather all the severed red pompon heads." A fine man he was. He could whistle any song" Tita was thinking aloud, rocking the broken flowers and the file tightly against her chest, on the verge of the precipice where her past stood and I was by it seeing her pain for the first time. I took his file from under her grasp to read: Ernesto Móvar 1926-72. Suicide. Found hanging in his cell.

"Who was he, Tita, and why does he have my surname? "

"Your father Ana."

Ana and her messenger birds

"My father?" My voice had ascended from an empty heart. How round and wholesome it sounded to my untrained ear, "My father", how crisp and fresh its meaning had slept unused by us for generations and yet...how very welcome the warmth his title raised. "My father" whose faults or virtues I might have inherited.

"He would have never hurt a fly," Tita defended his memory, "... he talked of the great things he was going to do, his projects would create thousands of jobs, would improve living standards...if only..."

"But he had a weakness, didn't he?" I guessed a political opinion.

"A blemish in his wholesome self," she admitted.

"Was it that which drove him away?"

"I can't betray all the dead dear, it would not serve any purpose, not now." And that was all there was to know about my father...except the crime he had been accused of in those soiled files. The regime had him as a suspect, the usual suspect, like every Basque in Valencia was after the bus explosion that killed my mother and my grandmother...oh god he had not, he could not have, not my father...my mother...

"He didn't Ana, believe me I know..." She had followed my trail.

"Tell me then Tita, I need to know"

"You don't and it's better this way," and with that she came back to the strewn files.

We went on collecting the evidential papers in charged silence, intent on our gruesome task until it became obvious that order could not be restored; some folders had ended painfully empty, some were lumpy with soil between their pages, the least looked ruffled, while in the worst cases the front page suicides did not match the deaths reported inside them.

We stuffed them all back into the suitcase but could not close it because the ropes had given way and the locks had been broken by some other busybody.

"So that's why all the rope, charming!" Tita exclaimed.

"Charming indeed! We are in a very delicate situation Tita; if this case belongs to him alone, someone might be looking out for him by now, and if Antonio is someone's safe keeper, someone is looking out for us by now. Either way someone is bound to collect it …at some time."

"It all depends on what happens in the next few days…Even in death that bloody general is affecting our lives!"spat Tita Celia mistrusting the serendipitous life she had often relied on.

"We may have the three mourning days to organise something."

"We don't Ana, he heard your daughter tonight. We have to act before the country comes out of the shock, if we want to protect her from his scheming."

Oh, thoughts most evil that run ahead of reality!

"Do we have any relations outside Valencia Tita?"

"I don't think so… I don't know…I was only a child during the war."

"Didn't Grandma talk about her family?"

"We always avoided talking about the past. I'm so sorry!"

Ana and her messenger birds

"What about Valencia, do you know anyone who might put you up for a few days?" Here my aunt hesitated and blushed.

"Let me think, I...we lost contact a few years ago, since the bomb but ...(at this she became agitated, awkward) I still remember the address from the days when I patronised the annual shoe fair. It is a private address, belonging to an old friend, "she confessed blushing.

There had always been a certain aura of mystery about the personal life of my good aunt that far from staining her reputation had lent her an air of superiority among the lesser mortals who knew her.

"Are you welcome there without previous notice?"

"There will not be anyone in, not anymore," she sighed with a heavy heart." But I still have access to it."

"I will take you there tomorrow with Aurora."

"Better off if you take us to the train station. I can manage the rest of the journey and that way you will not have a secret to keep or to give away...in case..."

Could there be a more protective mother than my dear aunt?

Next day dawned reluctantly. The morning chorus of domestic noise rose slowly, fearful of awakening the dead, and the dying. Leaded cumulus clouds trampled over rooftops on their downhill descent from the summit of the mountain and cats and dogs preferred to busy themselves indoors. The death of Franco was announced by his Prime Minister, in a lengthy eulogy bordering on the fanatical. Many shops stayed closed and they remained so for the following three days, out of fear of the possible national unrest and the probable chaos and looting taking place in similar circumstances, not for respect for the General as it was reported.

We packed a few necessities for Aurora and Tita for short stays and walked to the station. Those days and because of the petrol prices, we hardly used the car; only when there was no other transport available, also because our minuscule Seat 600 was incredibly old. We had nicknamed him "Uncle Paco" like the alias young people gave Franco because it was small, decrepit and it had been hanging on, threatening to die on us for years but never had actually broken down. It also had become unreliable for which we thought that it might die with Franco that day as its namesake and we did not want to use it in the vital errand we were undertaking.

With the neighbours we met on our way, we just exchanged a few greetings or incidental monosyllables as curtly as the occasion dictated. There was no loitering aimlessly that morning, or extended commentaries about an ailing gallbladder here and a chronic pain there. The routine rhetoric of village life was harnessed under a contrived taciturnity. It was tacitly understood that if we all kept our heads under the parapet for long enough, someone in Madrid would come up with the political solution to our new problem, to avert political upheaval, to reconcile all Spaniards and all grievances to avoid a second civil war, another carnage.

Hush, hush little children while the beast sleeps.

Ana and her messenger birds

But it was easy to keep quiet; after all, what were three or thirty days compared with thirty-six years of keeping quiet, of colluding by fault or default?

I am sure we all observed a cautious code of practice, the innocent and the guilty, the oppressed and the oppressor as one. Both sides of the nation were hurriedly burying the past, or what little of it remained lying around in the open, which could not have been interred until the death of the General.

That morning Tita and I arrived at the station a few minutes early unhindered by long conversations on the way up, with Aurora in my arms still sleepy. There was a minor evacuation taking place under the watchful eyes of the two "guardiaciviles", who were observing the hustle and bustle on both platforms in opposing directions, to Valencia and Madrid, with studied detachment. One was nibbling a toothpick while his partner tried to summon the due authority behind his green tinted sunglasses "a la americana". They were patrolling the north platform to Madrid as ever, as was usual in their daily round, and as always, they kept pace with each other, keeping strength in numbers.

Fellow travellers of all sorts came onto the Valencia platform through the gate, surveyed the ever-growing crowd, acknowledged the guards' presence and invariably adjusted their coats, stopped near the ones they knew best and found the weather and distant relations a good source of conversation. Hector, the plumber to our right, resented the approaching winter with venom, while his interlocutor was going to Valencia to collect his widowed sister. Marta, the matron constantly crossing her cardigan over her voluminous bosom, was "visiting mother" who was convalescing at the Provincial Hospital, "before the weather closed in" she added with a gentle nudge at my ribs. I nodded at decent intervals prolonging our one-way dialogue, holding my sleepy Aurora tighter in my arms. Tita Celia listened to the complaints that the other shoe merchant in town had about the new fashion on platform shoes, which had a longer life than the old stilettos, which made them less profitable; to which she answered that the problem might be soon worsened when men found they wanted them as well, to keep up with taller women, and between lament and complain the not- so- tall shoe seller was hypnotised by the oscillations of Tita's white plait tastefully resting over her ample bosom.

The only train to Valencia that day whistled in the distance provoking a myriad of meaningful stolen glances in all present.

Aurora became restless in my arms, perceiving my distress though unaware of the adults' reality. She had been unusually quiet all morning watching us pack. I patted her back and kissed her woolly hat, from which a few auburn curls had escaped and repeated the agreed story that she was going to Valencia to the fair to see the new giant carousel by the river, and Tita would also take her to the zoo.

And the train arrived...

I entrusted my daughter to my aunt and let the train swallow its precious cargo in deep silence.

The crowd was accommodated with undue docility, there were no queue jumpers, ticket dodgers or bogus pensioners. No, there was an unprecedented order that startled the two guardiaciviles and a swiftness in the two minutes that bordered on dexterity, with the ease of an over rehearsed final act.

I beheld my daughter's face through the coach window and waved back to her sitting on my aunt's lap, while the clouds coursed the sky as they had done many autumn mornings before. The station master whistled, the train whistled back and departed toward the hill side where it whistled a second time before entering the tunnel and it whistled a third time exiting the hill, as it had always done…and there came not a sign that something was amiss, a mere hint in the nature of that particular morning unsettling the heart, a harbinger, a preternatural voice from the town's dead and missing. It was not to be in my case; it being an ordinary series of events in serendipitous procession whilst I was unaware.

Malign impotence of ignorance!!

11 TWO TERRIBLE DEEDS

Two days of national mourning had passed and the same state of affairs gravitated around the suitcase, left covered under a blanket in the vestibule, like an unwanted visitor. The young prodigal prince and future king had in contrast become a guest of honour for whom the country was prepared to forget, if not to forgive; he was crowned in haste while I remained in limbo, unable to join in the euphoria, without news from my aunt or Antonio.

Oh, the paradox confounds the natural laws of justice!!

Night had descended on that second day of mourning uneventful and cold. A veil of frost which had hovered all day over the summit of the mountain had materialised in town with the last light of the evening, covering the ground as that last light left it but I had not noticed the cold or loneliness because I had been counting the hours, the minutes, the seconds, the beats of my own heart, the folds and rings of the curtain in the living room, the granite slabs in the vestibule...while at the same time in an unconscious mode I concocted different answers for all the possible questions he might ask about the suitcase and he could be anyone because someone was bound to reclaim such delicate luggage. To avoid that debilitating feeling of foreboding I began humming an old nursery rhyme:

"Now that we are strolling along,

Let us tell a few little lies…

In the sea swims the hare,

On the mountain the sardine, tra-la-ra…"

A slight tapping at the door had me running out of the sitting room into the vestibule. Though it was not his habitual call, his ominous presence had penetrated the ancient oak doors, for which I opened the door in deliberate darkness, letting the frosted night light shine upon his suitcase to direct him to our business without preamble; an invitation he acknowledged and followed, picking his heavy load and turning back on his heels for the second time in forty-eight hours. But the action was left unfinished when passing by me he sensed my dread. He stopped and sounding the air for noises and scents, realised that I was alone at home.

"Are you alone?" he enquired, still facing the waiting open door, absorbing my breath and my perspiration.

"Yes."

"And my daughter?" he asked in a steely voice, closing the door with deliberate calm.

"Tita took her to the specialist in Valencia" and there was a meditative pause in which I stepped backwards, and he set his luggage down.

"Have you opened it Ana?" and I said " No" because we truly had not. The rope had given way.

"You are saying that you don't know what it contains?"

"No" I said, hoping that it might have been disturbed before by the person who broke the locks.

"So, if I open it... when I open it, I will see my property intact...as I packed it?"

My early resolution began to quiver against his bluff, which I could not call that second time in our lives, not having seen how the contents originally lay. Oh, I needed my aunt by my side to help me lie convincingly.

"It fell...opened...when we were taking it upstairs." I uttered, stepping backwards once more, feeling the bannister in my back.

"You know what's inside," his statement felt like a sentence.

"But we'll never bother you at all Toni. Whatever you did or do is not my business. I'll never...tell a soul...I promise you!"

"I bet you do!!!" he hissed, advancing towards me with menacing calm, more felt than seen in the semi-darkness of a clear night, guided only by the brightness of my blouse, which in the acquainted penumbra of the hall was an unfortunate beacon.

"Are you as thin as you ever were or has motherhood rounded you a bit?" he slurred with a lascivious droll taking me by surprise because I had not foreseen that particular turn of events and I was not prepared...but some ancestral memory alerted me of what was coming next, so I turned to the bannister at the foot of the stairs and began to run for the safety of my room. He ran after me throwing lustful threats in the dark, so close at my heels that I had no time to lock my door.

And he raped me.

He raped me to sow the seed of fear in my body and mind.

What can be said of an act of such perversity without sinking into clichés that obscure and dilute the gravity of the action? There are no adjectives to describe a violation like there are no words to explain the pain of giving birth or the loss of death. I did not lose my honour or my innocence and neither did I lose it to a stranger.

But that night I lost my peace, all chances of future happiness, my trust. He touched my conscience with dirty hands.

That night in my room I looked for God, but he was not there. I cried for His help, but He did not assist me in my hour of tribulation. I cried aloud but neighbours did not interfere in domestic violence. I cried a second time, but he had stifled my screams with his hand. An odour foreign to myself permeated every inch of my skin. The scent which lovers relish turned nauseating in my memory. Instead of submitting to minimise the ordeal, I had resisted, and inadvertently prolonged the assault.

He left in the dark, as he raped me, and in the dark I emptied my wardrobe and dresser into the corridor and with only the filtering moon light from the shutters I locked the door of my room, so I might never step in by the force of habit to face the sickness he had left in my body, in my mind and bed. I showered and scrubbed my body and my scalp and went to my aunt's room; there I slipped in and curled inside her bed until she came back the next afternoon.

Ana and her messenger birds

When my shaking stopped, I began to thread coherent thoughts through the chaos in which I have been left, but the degradation inflicted had no reason to be. It was a hollow victory for him. A simple threat to the welfare of Aurora would have worked wonders, and he must have known it or experienced its effect before, by the contents of his suitcase.

That night I went to sleep in my aunt's bed with the bedside lamp on, as I have done since, fearful of the dark.

Damn him, damn him and his corrupted being, forever more.

How could the God of our doctrine have allowed the son of His creation to hurt me so aimlessly?

Wasn't I His daughter too? It was that night when I finally gave up His parentage and I have never since looked back to see if He was there, that is…until the day you came back to me ill, Ed.

My aunt returned from her hiding place the next afternoon at dusk and climbed into bed with me, where we cried loosely embraced, oblivious of the other's distraught state, weeping and hiccupping in alternative waves of despair. It was only when there were no more tears in our heaving, and when my eyes began to prickle with the swelling, that I noticed the childless silence about us. It parted the length of my spine in two with the coldness of a still blade when I asked the already known.

"Where is Aurora?"

"He has taken her away…I couldn't stop him. He caught us having breakfast…he let himself in somehow, and I could not run off or hide with our girl. Oh, it was all too horrible…too fast. I could not react in time. The old couple that came in with him acquainted themselves with Aurora, while he made me pack her things. Our little girl! He is using our girl as his guarantee, he told me, and warned us that she shall live happily so long as he feels secure on his way up the political greasy pole."

"How did she take it?"

"It was dreadful. We clung to each other by the foot of the bed, listening to the enticing offers of the old couple, watching them produce toys and sweets as if from a magic hat, and hearing Antonio threaten me in a coded language. I begged Ana. I pleaded until the old couple nearly gave in, but he did not quiver. He is a heartless man with many corpses behind his ambition. I am so very sorry dear Ana. I have done you a terrible disservice. What is it about me? First my sister, and now your daughter, I let them go."

"You did your best Tita." I tried to comfort her without understanding her double lamentation as I know now about the death of her sister, while I found it hard to cope with my anger Ed, because if my daughter had died, though unnatural to bury one's offspring, I would have known how to grieve, but to lose her that way, to have her taken from me, to imagine her pining for us and all that was familiar to her, to know her alive but inaccessible in order to preserve her very life, I was faced with an unwanted existence."

"How did he find you?" I asked, trying to make some sense of our situation.

"They must have had a file on me all these years."

"Why?" I asked, not knowing then about the hidden lives of

my relatives.

    "For sympathising with sympathisers, I suppose…but…why are you in my bed?" She changed our topic of conversation, throwing me off the scent of something more sinister, and I did not notice, Ed. If I had insisted…I might have learnt the truth about how I came to be, or known the secret address of my daughter's last innocent days."

"Why aren't you in your bed Ana?" Tita insisted.

    "I…I…he attacked me when he came for his suitcase," I said, coming back to my sobbing.

    "Did he …touch you…force you….? Oh, the evil in him will destroy us.

    "It shall not Tita. We must find Aurora. Who can help us?"

    "None of the signatories within his suitcase will be interested in hearing what they already know, they presume or have instigated. Think twice Ana before making public any of his crimes or our predicament."

    "I shall find my daughter by myself on the quiet, sooner or later. Spain is changing Tita."

    "That's why he is bound to take good care of her. She'll be alright as long as we do not attempt to expose him and if democracy comes as we have been promised, nobody will help us during the transition, the past will be buried."

    "I will see her again or I shall die of desolation. Will you help me Tita?"

    "I shall…tomorrow…Now I am so very tired. If only I could sleep forever and forget what I have done to you."

    "Shush! Do not mortify yourself with silly ideas. We will

find solutions tomorrow as you say. Now go to sleep..."

"Yes...Spain will get better...tomorrow will be a new day." And she fell asleep.

But the following morning came and found me alone in the world.

The stanchion, which had supported my somehow accidental moorings, had passed away during the unconscious hour. She had fallen asleep under a heavy conscience; her heart not having found the strength to beat beneath its oppressive burden of guilt at having come back without my daughter, gave in, capitulated.

But her sleep so desired had cheated her of her promised peace. Death had not lifted her distraught appearance, for her expression was tortuously fixed. Her lips had shrunk to a thin purple line. The leftovers of her makeup had dried like a riverbed, with lines and cracks strewn across her cheeks and mien. Her hand had set rigidly around my father's file scrolled within her grip, which she must have taken from the suitcase.

She was very cold, very unlike her former self.

There was a murmur blowing the curtains very gently, caressing the red geraniums and all the lace in the room. The murmur grew, and I could hear Grandma's voice as she used to say, "A woman should always go out looking her best." That voice was compelling for the love it had in it.

I jumped off her bed and began the ritual. I had to compose her appearance before the eyes of strangers were set on her undignified corpse, 'as she would have done for me', with meticulous care, with the same affectation she used to display when she performed her ablutions for me as a child. I chatted her up, with the same soliloquies she indulged in when bathing me in yesteryears. When she was done, and dressed in a purple dress she and Grandma had chosen years ago for the occasion, I cut one of the red geraniums she loved so much, and threaded it through her white hair, and this lent a tremulous blush to her marmoreal cheeks. I stepped back for a better view, and noticed that the touches seemed to agree with her former splendour, before our mothers died. Then, and only then, after surveying that her room looked as she would have wanted, and after the murmuring breeze stopped ruffling the geraniums, I called the doctor. He came to verify what Tita and I already knew, but had not admitted to, 'that she was dead' though he told me that 'she had left us'. He who had had a sheltered life under the regime, who had grown fat and blind to certain realities, and had put his signature in the death certificate of some of those wretched files, by the " found hanging" and "fell in the lake and drowned" statements, he was playing with euphemisms, as if my aunt had lived or died dishonourably; to which I replied before I could think, that "She had not, she would never have left me." So he rectified, "She has passed away Ana," while I kept shaking my head in denial." She is deceased child," he conciliated, to which I retorted, " my aunt is DEAD doctor, and that is the only reason she is not with me anymore, she is dead, and has died of a broken heart...and that shall be read in her death certificate, she didn't 'fall in the water and drown'."

We looked at each other across the distance separated by

the bed, in mutual disgust of the beast that we had all fed by commission or by omission for three decades. I held his stare with a blind determination to God-knows-what. He measured my intentions and my grief, our past, his future in the new Spain and loosened his mourning tie with his right index finger.

"She was the angel we all needed, and she has died of a broken heart," I repeated.

"That shall be it then," he said, closing his gabardine, and letting himself out in a whirlwind.

Then and not before, the tide began to flow dragging me away from my moorings, and the more I cried, the more dead she turned to me, stretching that tether which had made us one. That sleeping Ophelia floating in a pond of white linen and lace had once been in love…and she had looked after the family of her mother…and the daughter of her sister, like the best man around, and she had managed to preserve the radiance of a newlywed. Her jovial deportment never proclaimed the burdens she carried. Her undulating voice had invested me with a phenomenal repertoire of literary stories and anecdotes, but had deprived me of family secrets, perhaps to protect my childhood; however those blank spaces in the past of my family were aggravating the loneliness I felt standing there, by her bed, feeling the tether stretch some more and break. I was alone. My daughter was also alone.

And cry I did with gusto.

I wept with torrential noise.

I bellowed like a mourning animal.

Ana and her messenger birds

I cried to my heart's content,
And after that…
I cried myself to despair,
And to no avail I sobbed,
That there isn't an antidote for pain,
Other than crying after a good cry.

I felt powerless to stop myself from crying and indifferent to the sorry spectacle I must have offered to the friends and neighbours who came to the wake. I refused the tranquillisers in fear of losing that pain in my chest, afraid that without the suffering I would not pay the price for being left alive, for having willed events so wrongly.

Friends and neighbours suffered with me for a while and agreed that my estranged husband was 'this' and 'that' and fed me hen consommés and dyed my clothes for mourning but eventually, one quiet day, they all went back to their lives. It was impossible not to; with the unprecedented changes that were taking place, at a pace quicker than expected, without the feared mass hysteria, in the sobering knowledge of what might happen otherwise. But I had no life left to come back to. Prince Juan Carlos was crowned. A constitution was commissioned to be drafted by many men from differing ideologies and walks of life to be ratified by us the Spanish people, elections would be held, and political retaliations would not take place. There would not be truth and reconciliation trials because after nearly forty years evidence had become anecdotal and guilt was so widespread that it would have involved more than half of the population.

All had come too late for Tita Celia.

Ana and her messenger birds

It was during that winter that I took to baking those delicious chocolate cakes, sweeteners of my childhood in times of great upset and I made them like Tita Celia had done them in her turn when her mother had died. Like her, I had not been taught the secrets of their making, neither had I been given the magic recipe; however, a familiar image was conjured up in the mind after lighting the oven. I could visually count the spoonfuls of sugar that Grandma and later Tita used to pour into the mixing bowl. Tita's wrists were gently twisting right, left, right to separate the whites from the yolks. The vision progressed with my preparations: the busy rustling of a black pair of slippers accompanied the two older pairs of hands of my grandmother, counting the flatly loaded spoonfuls of flour as they fell with snowy effect onto the sugared yellow mixture, one...two...three...four...twenty...one short and a sad disillusion...one too many and an indigestion. Then she opened the hot oven and introduced her elbow, this time counting backwards, three...two...ouch! It's hot for chocolate; thus, I enacted what I have seen performed innumerable times to an exquisite perfection. After it, came the pleasure of eating it. Coded messages from before my birth. That particular cake and its making spoke to me of the secret language of my predecessors, it fortified the vacuous hours of my first winter alone. It brought me strength and fed my determination to find Aurora; if only to see that she was well looked after."

"And did you find her Ana?" Ed pressed me to continue.

"I found her one April afternoon like this, living in a suburb of Madrid, though not by accident after five arduous months of concealed search, deceiving friends and neighbours, travelling to and fro at weekends to corroborate evidence, to check addresses and names using my marriage certificate, with the suspicion that the old couple my aunt had talked about were Antonio's parents probably duped into their part in the kidnapping. From then on it all depended on how well I remembered some of the official names in the notorious suitcase, to avoid their area of influence."

"My reward for my long wait was Aurora herself, dressed in radiant yellow under her school blue pinafore, engaged in conversation with one of her playmates, whispering in each other's ears in intimate camaraderie, by the low fence in the playground. Her auburn hair had been loosely plaited to celebrate her generous features, her almond eyes, her tomboyishness. She was already taller than the average six-year old, for which her whole attire had been handcrafted to fit her to perfection. I felt eternal gratitude to the loving hand that was toiling behind my daughter's obvious contentment; even though the image of a reciprocal love wounded me mortally with the darts of oblivion."

"I had to make a Solomonic decision."

"Some mothers have lost their offspring to death or disease, many to marriage, others to religions or wars and their wishes had not been an option in such fates; whereas I let her go to save her from harm (real or supposed), so we might meet again in more propitious circumstances. Between her suffering and mine there was no choice. I had no control over the actions and interests of everyone involved in our situation, but I could hide my discovery to keep in contact from afar."

"As it happened, with careful planning and one day drives at odd times, I continued visiting my daughter in complete anonymity until the failed military take-over of 1981,when I began to receive anonymous threatening letters; that was the last I saw of Aurora who was by then eleven years old."

A very long pause in my narrative allowed the clock on the mantelpiece to chime twelve incongruous times reverberating over the furniture therein. I had brought memories back from the nether parts of my past to my present life in England, to Ed, and the living room was swarming with all the imagery I had involuntary invoked: my long gone relations in various sizes, ages and attires, artefacts and other memorabilia long time forgotten…and a few demons. The images carrouselled around us in a silent macabre waltz. Ed was bemused. I managed to stay calm. We looked at each other across that multitude of spectres. I resisted the temptation of running away, shocked by some of the scenes that passed between us, until the ghostly dance gradually exhausted its natural spin and all images great and small, benign and malign orderly went back to where they belonged.

Ed held my hand to say, " I see you have mastered your past," but I remained quiet, for what is it to master one's past? To grow detached from it, to put it in perspective. How could I disassociate my present from my past when my feelings, ideas, reasoning, and natural reactions were the result of it?

But I noticed that thinking about it did not hurt me with the same intensity of when it was fresh, though the deeds had not changed after their completion. I had not registered that imperceptible change in me, and it frightened me. It unsettled me that my feelings had moved on without my consent and that lack of unbearable hurt made me feel a deserter.

"Don't worry Ana, life is volatile. That is what is so beautiful about it, it permutes to accommodate our survival…most times."

THE AUCTIONED GERANIUMS

The following day after lunch, Ed and I decided to spend the remaining warm hours doing some tentative gardening. With the events of yesterday, the lawn had not improved as the rest of the garden had, so it had to be rescued somehow. Ed carried on his lap the step-by-step wonder book of gardening while I wheeled him to the patio, but there was as far as we advanced with our gardening chores, because the grass had come to life by itself. A dense carpet of emerald green blades shone under the caress of the sea breeze with undulating effects.

Nature alone, with the myriad of miracles she performed every spring, could not have engineered that funfair of green shades in just one night.

"Do you see what I'm seeing?" I asked Ed, approaching our novel Eden, to which he whistled an affirmative "yea" appraising the grand floral display in front of our eyes. The bloom and foliage of the four seasons within that timid spring afternoon: all plants, tubers, bulbs and seeds that I had planted, buried and sown in the last two years and had never come to fruition, had appeared at last. Red hot pokers competed with bluebells and wild strawberries. Spring flowering trees rivalled the exuberance of passion flowers and Russian vines, tumbling generously over the fences.

But our apparent paradise had not reached the two corners at either side of the back gate. A mossy winter had set at the left of it, being mid-autumn to the right of that prodigious gate. Through it came the taciturn figure of my aunt Celia, toward what seemed her autumnal plot at the right by the foot of the hill and there she kneeled down and rested her hands in her lap, staring silently at the dying oleander bush which was mortally plagued by yellow scorpions, seeming yellow itself…of a putrid quality.

"You have to help her out of her purgatory Ana," Ed pleaded for Tita Celia. I parked him near the edge of the garden, to keep him as a spectator, then I walked to her side. Ed was still advising from his chair" Tell her about Aurora Ana, that might be it!" I sat on the ground by her side in absent contemplation, like herself.

"I found Aurora, Tita," both of us contemplating the dying oleander, avoiding looking into each other's eyes.

"Was she well?"Her voice was thick with emotion.

"She was staying with her grandparents…they have given her the care and devotion we would have been proud of, in better circumstances."

"Did he ever harm her…or you again?"

"Never Tita, neither of us have seen him since but I did hear of his political ascent from time to time." To this she paused and weighed her next question. " Are you happy,

Ana and her messenger birds

Ana?"

"…No Tita… and you, are you…were you actually happy?"

" I did what I chose to do, which is more than my contemporaries did."

" And no regrets?"

"I had to do it… a matter of conscience if you must know, and I had my reward with you and your daughter, caring for you two, having you near."

Many of the yellow creatures feeding off the oleander began to die with contorting spasms, dropping systematically onto the sodden ground, like autumnal leaves. Tita Celia sighed with relief and proceeded in a haze," My geraniums…?"

" I brought one of them to England with me, as you would have wished."

She levelled her eyes with the oleander bush in a pensive manner and murmured," My geraniums have a long history you must know, going back nearly half a century to the night of St. John on midsummer's night…", and there she paused to create the necessary intrigue very much in her old manner of history telling. I glanced at Ed. His body exuded life, a certain quality of life, a borrowed thirst for the unknown but anticipated drama had permeated his enfeebled frame; his cheeks glowed with contained curiosity for a past half known half presumed. A short allusion to a midsummer's night was sure to keep us waiting for a broken romance. The spoils of death had not diminished Tita's temperament.

She continued her musings in a remote tone: " The shortest night to dream of pagan games, when our nine-year old post-war was dragging up its rank hills at the pace of an ailing turtle, though that fact was not an obstacle to street parties but the reason. It was another long-awaited time for escapism, of self-delusion, of leaving worries behind, rationing books, disappearances, and chronic hunger. It was the hour for a romantic interlude, of such naïve intensity as to feed the next twelve months preceding the following midsummer's night.

It was summer in its early hours, of bearable temperatures at lunchtime and warm nights of honey- suckle scent. We had not seen an orange since before the war but all the same... the town square shone under hundreds of light bulbs strung around the perimeter, like in times of plenty. From every standing pole, streetlamp and balcony hung verbena baskets as if to ratify the nature and name of those gatherings known as "Verbenas". The podium erected for the occasion lay in readiness since the night before, wrapped in a lengthy cloth of patriotic colouring. Lavender sprigs had been strewn over the square signalling the importance of the event, following a mediaeval tradition of obscure origins.

The musicians had arrived from various villages, in the spontaneous ensemble that preceded the provincial tour of festivities, having no set fee except the fortuitous takings of the auction bouquets which opened the 'verbena' of St. John's dance and others. Young men of all backgrounds had settled around the tables of the bars and cafes dotting the square, to wait in amiable society, laced coffee in hand, for the feminine arrival traditionally late and in small groups or pairs. The feminine congregation poured young grace in perfumed waves from every converging street into the plaza and the men, having patiently waited for hours, became restless and boisterous. He was there already, among a liberal crowd of marriable men, tall, of intense mien and lazy walk, and he attracted oblique glances from both sexes who, used to the local features and traits of manly beauty, felt wary or aware (invariably) of his outlandish distinction, his northern accent, his perennial espadrilles.   But I recognized my Guernica in the newcomer. His scent was that of my native Basque country, his eyes had recently seen what mine remembered but vaguely. My roots were a pale reflection of his fresh northern-ness; while I had lost much of our native culture over years of Valencian town-life, he still preserved a foreign remoteness, even in the way he held a glass of wine to his lips, slow, appreciative, and quiet. He had arrived with an army of workmen and other engineers for the repairs to the road leading to the Buseo dam, to the west of Baños, high up in the valleys that carved their way through the mountainous provincial border between Requena and the west of Valencia.

He had found lodgings with Doña Inés but despite her laborious tongue and her many social skills, he still remained a mystery after three months of local curiosity and scrutiny. Our paths had crossed a dozen times, never chancing more than a 'Hi'? 'Hiya?'; and only recently I had sold him a pair of leather shoes (which he never wore) and yet ...I acknowledged his glances longer than chaste civility advised, and cherished them, and hid them from the mundane chatter. Wherever we happened to meet, accompanied or alone, he held my stare undeterred by my height pleasantly overshadowed by his own and he caressed my longings bringing my heart to a frenzied gallop. His grace on doing so was unaffected, perhaps unknown to him who appeared to be in constant thought and maintained a quiet camaraderie with everybody. There seemed to be scores of girls and young women Rosa, my young sister had whispered, who had amorous designs on my foreigner, to which I could only sigh… and sigh again, for I had never had a romantic crush on any boy or man, nor great expectations; only that maddening urge to befriend my northerner and not knowing how. St John's Ball was a propitious venue one would be tempted to say, if one had not perceived my height in flat shoes, dwarfing all prospective dancing partners, hence I had always danced in the background camouflaged by the multitude, where girls danced with other girls.

Such an undignified state of affairs had not bothered me before and the thought would have passed me by if the new engineer had not come to town, if his temperament had not excited mine, if his silences had not been so appealing …if I had not fallen in love against my own advice.

That evening I had taken extra care with my hair, piling high loop over loop in a fashionable soft construction, in my last attempt to pursue what I did not know I would soon have to give up. I even wore high heel sandals in the knowledge that my scaffold would deter other minor suitors, but that night it would be him… or no one else. His would be the image of my idle hours in my dull nights, the sustaining warmth in the winter of my life; his memory would be my fortitude in difficult times.

I would never be alone again.

No Ana, no, your assumption does not do me justice. I had never acted upon my impulses or wilfully manipulated situations to suit my wishes; mine was a matter of life and death, though I could never have guessed that what had commenced as my last swan song, would bring widespread disaster to all concerned.

It was of the public dominion that I would never marry. I had serenely accepted my destiny, when my sister Rosa was diagnosed with recurring and worsening fits. It became obvious to all in town that I, with a steady position, might be the man lacking in my family.

I used to wonder from time to time during my teen years, how would Ana have acted had she been alive instead and tried rigorously to follow what would have been her code of conduct: it had been my hand that mother had grasped in the treacherous river current, leaving me to cope with Ana's misfortune or sacrifice. Either way, hers had been an ephemeral agony, mine would last a lifetime of spinsterhood. Alas! I was not made of the kind of substance martyrs are made of. The fine veneer of my most noble pledges did not disguise my human condition, my awakening womanhood.

If I could only taste my forbidden dream!

That eve of the Verbena the mirror in the upstairs landing attracted us with unusual magnetism. Rosa and I had been in a trance since the afternoon, seemingly busy but stealing interminable flights of fancy at its reflection. When we were finally ready, composed and perfectly arranged like bouquets of fresh flowers, we formally confronted our reflections as a fait-accompli; what had not been achieved in five hours would remain so forever and what perfection was attained would be short-lived, though it had a pleasing effect to last the evening.

"Green suits your ways, Celia," Rosa observed me through the looking glass. Side by side, hand in hand, we examined the life-sized mirror, spellbound not for what we saw in it but by our own high expectations on that one night.

"Blue becomes you Rosa" and we gazed further into our own reflection, never minding mother's comings and goings around us, tidying the debris of a long makeover.

"Oh Celia, I would sell my soul for the honour of opening the ball tonight."

"And what will you do tomorrow when you wake up soulless?"

"I would not care!"

"But I would," I said, pressing her against me.

"We may never have a husband, but our soul and thoughts will always be ours."

"What will I do with them for the rest of my life, eh, tell me?"

"You will know what to do when the time comes; meanwhile I will look after you, agreed?"

"But it is a husband I want, to take care of me, Celia."7

"Only a special man will do for you Rosa. Don't lose yourself to a chimaera, promise me?"

"Big words will not placate my longing Celia."

"What about Maria 'La Bella'? Do you hear her laughing

nowadays? Does she love that brute of a husband after her Saturday beatings, eh? No, my girl, she does not…or Marcela, slaving for the tribe of in-laws she married into, does she walk sprightly like her former self or does she drag her feet in a ghostly fashion nowadays?"

"I find the engineer very, very interesting, Celia."

"Many of us think alike," I admitted blushing.

"Have you forgotten Marcela and her tribe?" Rosa niggled me through the mirror.

"His family lives conveniently far up north in Guernica," I elaborated further, unwittingly.

"My, my, you have done your homework."

"Privilege of my job," I teased mischievously, and we continued our light exchange through the mirror for a while, holding each other's waist, making sure we were not unsophisticatedly early.

"I must tell you Ana that your mother and I were very close when young. The same tragedies that precipitated her illness during the war had bound our blood ties…and unfortunately led to our late estrangement. It was uncanny that being nearly identical outwardly in measurements, hair and eye colouring, profile and size, our similarity was seldom perceived by even the closest scrutiny. Our different temperaments gradually distorted the family likeness, growing more and more apart as the years went on, until the physical similarities disappeared: with her illness worsening and other disorders setting on…you know, we are what we think, what passes through our minds, our likes and dislikes, passions and hatreds and we become strangers, impostors of our precious selves... but she was not to blame and neither was I dear Ana."

"Before I continue with my story and in fear of repeating myself, I have to say that I could never have anticipated the disastrous consequences of that St. John's Ball. Only your existence redeems all our deeds. But enough of the preamble and justifications and more of this my post-mortem expiation.

The truth has been long overdue for your sake dear Ana. If only..."

More scorpions fell from the branch of the oleander.

"In the plaza the squalor of the late forties had been dressed in its Sunday best," Tita continued. "The church was bolted, lest the pagan spirit without may corrupt the sanctity within. The town hall's marbled-front had been polished, the remainder of the facades in the square exhibited a fresh coat of whitewash, and the men...were waiting."

"The musicians were consuming those last minutes testing their archaic brasses and wind instruments, which seemed better tended than their monochrome flannelette suits but their precarious ensemble passed unseen, as usually obscured by the magnificent bouquet of live flowers on display, courtesy of Miss Elena, who put her horticultural talents at the service of all. "

"The auction began its usual ceremony with the accurate routine and pandemonium much loved by the mayor turned auctioneer for the evening. A floating whisper spread like a fountain about the feminine congregation to the left of the stage; it increased and decreased intermittently with each bid, and it rose to a cricket-chorus as the bidding reached last year's limit. Then the race to the highest bid slowed its pace and bidders were thinned out. Some cautious young men abandoned the game, giving up their chance to pick and choose their heart's desire, in favour of a less demanding girl. They would try again at the next St. John's, and would persevere to no avail, marrying all the same, the most accessible bride."

By ten o'clock only six men remained bidding, adding value to the bouquet. The engineer stood out amongst the half-a-dozen bidders scattered about the square. Carlos, the apprentice to an apothecary, hoped to dance with his long-standing sweetheart Maria Louisa, on her birthday. The fidgety redhead still counting his peseta notes felt an unrequited passion for my neighbour Elena. The fourth man and wearer of an American felt hat, had opened the ball a few times already with a different and younger girl each year and the other two…had yet to disclose their intentions 'honourable or not' under their well-cut suits and not very-well liked company; having been seen too often with the authorities and other undesirables. The trodden and crushed lavender strewn throughout the square inebriated the already excited minds and bodies, turning our hearts into the easy prey of romantic dreams, while the bidding continued.

"Twenty Reales on my right," squawked the Mayor on his rostrum, covered in sweat.

"Twenty five, " the redhead added, ogling at Maria Luisa with pride across the square.

"Thirty," shouted the victorious American hat wearer,

spurring a wave of "I-told-you-sos".

"Thirty five," minced proudly the well-tailored contender, of dubious connections.

"Forty," spat prouder still his comrade known locally as the undertaker, after the job he was reputed to keep in the secret police service.

"Fifty Reales," offered the engineer with an unmistakable northern accent, sending a wave of torrid air to every feminine throat. There was a natural pause as the bidders took stock of their possibilities and money and acknowledged their positions in the stunned crowd. The sum was larger than any other ever taken by the illustrious quintet in a musical get-together, thus they also became restless over the suspended motion of all there present.

Rosa exchanged a meaningful look with me. Mari Luisa lowered her head lamenting the loss of her birthday present. The multitude hissed beneath the canopy of light bulbs, and the mayor wiped off a patina of sweat from his face and receding hairline, with an enormous handkerchief obliterating the whole of his head in the act.

"Sixty Reales" baritoned the American hat wearer, unwilling to admit defeat and confronted the tallest bidder with a daring look; he in turn gazed around, momentarily lost, until our eyes met across the murmuring public.

His tacit proposition received my mute agreement.

I had been asked to open the ball by the only man I would have danced with.

"Seventy Reales', my engineer pronounced in a deep velvety tone, more a private caress than a public announcement, leaving no doubt upon his unshakeable intention of having the bouquet of flowers that year. The hat wearer hesitated. The mayor coughed twice and ran a sticky finger under his collar. The crowd forgot the national squalor for a brief moment and asked for the stakes to be raised but the man with American tastes appeared to have lost interest. He resettled his hat deeper to his right side 'for the benefit of the cinema goers' and approached the better man to shake his hand with grandiloquent Hollywoodian gesture, meriting a satisfied uproar from the public; women applauded and men relaxed their tense frames because trouble had been averted once more. The guardiaciviles strewn in couplets near the entrances to the square lowered their guard and loosened their hold on their carabines, not without an oblique glance here and there.

"And who is the lucky lady? "asked the mayor through the megaphone, reluctant to give up his rostrum but he was ignored. My engineer advanced to the foot of it, honoured his debt, cut the head of the biggest red geranium of his purchased bouquet, and brought it to me.

"Will you dance?"

Will I dance?!

That was the moment I had been born for, the purpose of my surviving the river crossing, the substance of my future dreams. Reality ceased to mean the impediment of happiness. My conscience abated her eyelids for an eternal evening when his palm slightly pressing my back, guided me through the first dance.

The now prosperous five-some musical talents opened the

Verbena to the accords of the then popular Cole Porter, and we began the Beguine in the clearing made just for the first dancing couple.

"My name is Ernesto, but everyone calls me Nacho," he offered with a tremulous voice.

"Mine is Celia," I let out my breath to escape my shaking body.

"I know, CE-LI-A," he whispered in my ear and I closed my eyes to allow his voice to filter through my senses, through my skin, so I would remember the taste of those words during the barren winters that lie ahead of me; so certain to come as I was of his devotion in later years.

That evening we crossed the cultural summer solstice in a rhythmic embrace, oblivious to everything but the art of moving so close, feeling the contours of our bodies without real contact: it would have been improper to do so, you know? Which made the game more exciting when the accidental caress of a fortuitous dancing mistake or collision happened.

From that St. John's onwards there were no limits to our passion. That hunger for each other's company and the insatiable thirst for the other's voice did hurt and please as one indivisible emotion, elongating the empty hours of separation between meetings. A summer haze crept in our lives, through which I could not see my mother's disquiet and I failed to perceive my sister's misplaced affections and my lover's dangerous attachment to me. I lived for our evening walks after closing time at the shoe shop, for the Saturday visit to the cinema where his hand proved to be tender and his kisses (though furtive) they were generous. He did not rob caresses. He never took my lips, he never stole a kiss, his were offered or given and I did receive them without contrived decency, and I drank my sweet wine from the sacred chalice of his lips.

Oh, my sweet lover who smelt of arid land dampened under the first drops of a summer storm. My lover smelt of love, plain love, love without artifice, the kind of love that subjugates the strongest and enslaves the weakest. There is no known antidote against such a powerful affliction...but who was ever found to want its end while under its influence and power?

I did not.

I did not wish my heartache to cease, not during our romance, not the day I realised I could not go on seeing him deluding my destiny and not even after our parting did I want that bitter-sweet euphoria to stop hurting me.

I did not wish to do what I had to do, but many bad decisions are taken for the sake of others, at a very short notice, and out of character.

It was by chance that I came to the decision that autumn day, having taken it many years before; the exact time of accomplishment had never been set because it was taken for granted that that day might never arrive but it did...at my own volition. I had nurtured the only dream I should not have had, lived in a limbo for a time that was not mine alone and it brought misery upon my mother and sister.

It was by chance that I heard them conversing in Rosa's room (your room, Ana) and it was fortuitous that they never noticed my presence within the doorframe as they continued what seemed an habitual exchange, seated on the bed facing the window. And I listened despite my better judgement, not wanting to eavesdrop but unable to retreat unheard. Mother was soothing Rosa with conciliatory gestures, while chastising her for setting her heart on the wrong man." But it's the only chance she has to know the love she deserves, Rosa," mother entreated.

"But if she's not marrying, why does she entertain him, mother?"

"You know well why Celia shall not marry him or any other."

"Then why can I not love him if I wish to?"

"You might not marry either, my pet, not with your complaint."

"Oh, mother, you know I love her…but I love him too!"

"She will always take care of you Rosa. Do never forget her plight."

"I cannot hide what I feel forever, not while he's so near and free."

"His heart is not free. It will never be by the look of things…"

And Rosa broke into tears and convulsive pathos, bent over mother's ample black lap, on the brink of one of her fits, sadly rendering irrelevant mother's efforts to contain her suffering. Her baking hands stroked my sister's hair again and again, sighing at the window. I had not realised I was moving forward into the bedroom until mother looked up startled, caught in flagrant tenderness and immediately horrified that I might have overheard what I should not have; whether it was her championing of my cause or my sister's disloyal admissions that she was flustered about, I don't know, because she was not in the habit of loving openly, always discreet in her affections, and austere with her demonstrations of them since the day of the bombing. None of the three of us were used to the overwhelming emotions which had overcome our pale and limited existence since the mid-summer's night ball.

I could only look on feeling deprived of sane reasoning. "I just came in to tell you the latest and I must rush out," I blurted out, causing an explosion of noises and perplexed glances across the bed.

"What is it?" Mother was the first to react.

"Do you remember the secretarial course I was offered in April to qualify as manager in the shop, which I put off because of summer's late closing? Well, I'm enrolling in it…and finishing with Nacho. There, don't make me change my mind because we need a pay rise, don't we?"

Mother observed me intensely sorrowful and silent.

"Why?" dared my sister Rosa with a tear-stained face.

"We could take you to a private specialist…"

"No, why the other…Your business with Nacho?" and I could not find the appropriate words to elaborate on my hasty decision. I found it hard to breathe and think and lie all at once.

"Your sister will be studying evenings and weekends Rosa," mother offered in neutral tones that belied the turmoil of her eyes.

Ana and her messenger birds

"I have to go now mother...would you explain to Rosa?" I pleaded from the corridor, fleeing the scene.

"I will...and I will prepare a chocolate cake for supper."

Just like that. Now it is and now it is not, abracadabra; as if vital decisions were taken by the hour with emotional impunity but you see, mortal wounds were easy to withstand during the post-war years, when people were in the habit of inflicting them or receiving them. But nine years on, it was the constant corroding hurt and the merciless infliction of precious memories, what made life (at times) a dreary place, not the occasional mortal wound.

On the surface, we had managed to avert one of Rosa's fits, and had solved the question of my future with a sensible conclusion; though deep inside ourselves, the feeling of having just postponed the inevitable one more day prevailed. One sacrifice today and reward tomorrow to maintain the sense of humanity, perhaps to create the desired mirage that things were well. All the same, passions do not suddenly die and disappear; the energy is transformed into something else of dangerous and volatile nature and mother and I could not have predicted the change in my sister's new resolution.

13 A PARDONABLE TREASON

"Those were the secret origins of my red geraniums dearest Ana. They became a reminder of what your father and I had meant to each other, a memento I treasured lacking a more personal token for which your mother developed an irrational contempt."

"What about my origins, Aunt Celia?" I ventured causing more yellow scorpions to die on the oleander branches and drop on the ground. "Whose daughter am I?"

"I kept my word, Ana; you are your mother's daughter."

"But…I always imagined…you know, you and I are so much alike…"

"Your mother and I were very much alike once, before she deteriorated but it is my care that shows in your face."

"And you never…"

"Never with your father."

"What happened then?"

"Allow me to come back to the events of that summer and autumn."

Ana and her messenger birds

I do not know the reasons my mother found for my unexpected change of heart. I never asked her, but I had to go, to run out to breathe the October evening air because to stay would have left me exposed to my painful self. I also had to find Nacho and tell him what everyone else knew but him. I ran downhill through the maze of back streets and alleyways, prolonging the entrance in the square where Nacho would be waiting outside the Café Plaza. I needed to scheme and elaborate in detail the minutiae of gestures and reasons I should enact to make him hate me…or forget me quickly. I had seen it done in the movies, by Bette Davis. It seemed a generous and effective gesture and it looked easy. I could not allow him to suffer on my account for an event set in motion before we met. The thought of his unrequited love was unbearable; the more so, because I would never cease to love him while he might still love me from afar. Hope dies with indifference, as you know."

And there he was as usual, patiently waiting toying with his matchbox, oblivious of the passing feminine glances boring upon his serene countenance. From those steps at the Café Plaza, we started on our long walks to the various parks and promenades in which decent relationships were conducted but that evening would not see us in any of our accustomed venues. The errand I was about to undertake was easier conducted within the neutrality of open streets and witnessed by any passer-by; so that it might be a definitive end to the eyes of all and there might not be the chance of a last kiss or a comeback.

We started our ambling progress in a quiet mood. I hung

onto his right arm. We eyed each other at intervals side-by-side as we advanced on our way to nowhere. His warm body pulsated next to my left arm, in that disturbing but sweet way, innate of him and no one else.

(Oh, mother; forgive me for I could not poison his mind against me!)

"I have something to tell you Nacho," I started as we neared the set of alleyways preceding the old castle quarters.

"I don't want to hear," he pleaded with a bad presentiment. The evening milk maid approached us on her daily business, balancing her onerous churns and measuring wares with oriental dexterity. We exchanged neighbourly courtesies at the footbridge of the mediaeval fortress that had for centuries joined the upper and lower halves of the town, through a labyrinth of inhabited lanes and stepped tunnels.

"Do you know it then?" I asked when we were alone again.

"No, but… I do…and I rather I didn't, Celia."

"There is no future in what we feel for each other, Nacho."

He interrupted me with a flat monotone "What do you mean?" halting my way to search my furtive eyes beneath the shivering light of that autumnal evening, with the moon flooding my features. It was difficult to discern his own eyes from my illuminated angle; alas his grip on my elbows echoed the aching of the unsaid and unseen expression.

Oh, my dear Ana, why don't we listen to our better judgement? I could not have made him hate me. My earlier determination withered away. I did not pronounce any of the fabled reasons that would have turned me hideous to his unsuspecting nature; come what might (which it eventually did) but I could not contrive a crude image of myself while in the boundaries of this immediate pain. What resulted from our last rendezvous was that we were no more and would never be engaged, even though we would belong to each other forevermore, and that my sacrifice was only equalled by his renunciation. Thus, we forced ourselves to become acquaintances; the sort that only meet in public places to exchange trivialities because anything else would have aided our longing for our lost intimacy.

Thereafter we found in my sister a common cause by which the daily grind might be alleviated; a safe point of convergence in the metaphysic plane as her welfare became paramount to our exchanges when and where we happened to cross each other's paths.

During the winter months I changed the nature of my loving, to avoid any resentment against my sister. I grew to love her in my mother's way and to think of her needs as those of a child and so did Nacho through the daily exchange about her health and progress. One month followed the other and June came and found us around the same civilities.

"How are ties to be severed, if there's no visible thread there?"

The impasse in which our broken relationship seemed to subsist had begun to erode the character of my mother; whom having been earthly and understanding, had become watchful and taciturn, until I did not distinguish between her care and surveillance, not only on my behalf but on that of my sister. I too began to observe our domestic arrangement, noticing to my astonishment the changes in my sister. She was keeping odd times. Not that they were unsociable, but they were unusual times for her methodical nature. It became obvious to mother and me that she kept secrets from us but still we did not interfere, seeing that her fits had ceased, and her appetite improved. Also, her appearance had altered in imperceptible ways, owing it to some spiritual or mental change while there were no real physical differences.

Mother began to suffer from insomnia.

The summer grew to gather dust.

My encounters with Nacho became sporadic.

Mother burnt her first chocolate cake.

My pot of red geraniums prospered on my balcony.

I began to suffer from insomnia.

Mother confided her suspicions to me.

A man was behind our disquiet.

I…informed my mother of my premonition.

Notwithstanding the suspense, an agreement was reached by which we felt that we could not confront Rosa, with what might have looked like a product of my own jealousy and resentment but we would gather evidence before taking action; hence we took turns in our vigil for a week, at the end of which (and without previous intelligence) mother discovered the note over my sister's dresser. It was written with clarity and precision, executed by the steady hand of a determined will, well sure of the actions taken and the motives which promoted them. A missive of dreadful consequences, planted in the most conspicuous surface of the otherwise immaculate room, aired, dusted and swept daily and kept dark, depriving insidious dust particles of their travelling medium. The temperature of my sister's room never altered from day to night and from season to season, in the most sepulchral inactivity, which that white paper denounced with deliberate intent. It read:

Nacho and I are marrying today in Valencia. We are not eloping. I will not be his before the ceremony. Please do not worry. Nacho is going to take good care of me. When the time has blurred the gravity of our actions, we will come back to visit you. Promise. I pray that Celia forgives my secrecy; however, she must concede that her breaking with Nacho left him a free man and what else could I do but love him better in his tormented abandonment. I am in excellent health and contrary to your fears, love and marriage...and children...will keep me in good stead. I feel God is by my side.

Your loving daughter and sister, Rosa

"The fool!" mother lamented. "Silly girl, tricked by her own heart into a labyrinth of misfortunes. Her ruinous heart!"

"Mother, don't. Nacho shall look after her."

"As for him, what ill-fate has blown him to these parts, only God knows!"

"Mother, don't. Please. I still love him!"

"How can you after this?" She waved the white note in the air. "Have you no sense Celia?"

"He has not meant to hurt me, mother. Not intentionally. He is a better man than you credit him for, but sadly his heart has played him wrong. Very, sadly, very wrong."

"The heart...the bloody heart," lamented mother tearing the letter in tiny pieces as she recited ruefully to herself:

"The heart, what a necessary evil in our lives,
common malaise of anarchic tendencies
An organ of corrosive side-effects.
Incurable disease, the heart.
It will kill us all."

"Oh, mother, what are we going to do?"

"What can we do but wait?" she proffered scattering the papers all over the floor.

There is a limbo, a benign haven where infants wait to be delivered, where when the mind is disturbed we linger unwilling to leave, and where the very old amble intermittently in and out of it. A limbo where to wait in peace absent-mindedly and painless until the body and mind heal. But there was no such place for us.

The broken-hearted may do with long stretches of interminable hours, days and months, visits to the empty room and more waiting. Mother and I put our lives on hold for a year, not knowing what to think of the pair's silence; whether not having any news was good news, or if the later it came the news would be worse, which is what eventually happened.

During that time of ignorance, we endured her absence, still loving her from afar. I postponed my private tragedy until a better time came to deal with my lover's treachery.

We emerged from our inertia in the tenth month, and began to decorate the spare room in the vestibule, because upper floors and stairs are not safe for babies, and we lived with frenzied anticipation of the events that would bring us, not only our Rosa back, but her child also. An infant in a home had never been a concept envisaged to outlive our unmarried trio. That peculiar extravaganza at that time, bordered on the bizarre in Spain with the absence, until then, of an unthinkable paternal figure in the equation; moreover, now mother had excluded it from her traditional scheme of life. That empty chair in the family's imaginary photograph was a fact, because for mother, Nacho could only be a depraved man given the existent inter-relation between Rosa, him, and myself.

Of me...he would receive my pardon.

Having attempted to care for whom I cared most and having failed against the nature of her illness, he would bring her back to us (not abandoned) entrusting his child, you, to me. I was sure of this, though he never asked openly.

What if not my forgiveness for loving so tragically could he deserve, when I stood to gain everything he would lose? He could not divorce his disturbed wife, or live with her against her will, and our law would never allow him to remarry, no second chances. He would lose his baby, you, Ana, and my love. My empathy could be the only decent feeling I could outwardly afford him, in payment for his unfortunate, but misplaced good intentions to love me from afar in the person of my sister. He would procure me a child, his child; though I knew that that had not been the motive behind the white note. None of us could have foreseen the irrevocable deterioration of my sister's health or guessed the path that her fancies would lead her through. Her fits were only one of the effects of her condition. Something more sinister lurked behind her groundless rancour and changes of humour, to which we were never given a name and treatment, as it was not as serious as polio or malnutrition during the post-war, but which I was later to hear it referred to by various names, much later, much too late.

When the day came, the day that Ernesto brought Rosa back, we had had a year to rage, to hurt and twelve months of missing and not knowing, time to settle dust on the loss and prepare for the gains and we were eagerly expecting their arrival, grateful to him who had made us a family by losing his own in the process.

That June evening, we confronted our worst fears. There was an urgent knock at the door unlike that of neighbours or friends. Mother opened the door to be flattened by the avalanche of our prodigal Rosa and they both exploded in shrilling exclamations, pelting each other with tears and questions, reproaches and I-shouldn't-haves, to be swallowed by the vestibule, then the kitchen to the heart of our home, while I was left under the lintel wearing only a dash of love protruding through my circumstantial demeanour and my hollow hands. He was left on the other side of it, still tall and involuntarily graceful, still him, with you in his arms wrapped in white froth and eau de cologne. He did not cross the threshold. Forwarding his bundle into my empty hands, he barely said, "Rosa does not want us anymore, will you tell my daughter that I loved her?" But my voice had deserted me. Sensations and feelings were escaping us to reach the other. The bundle, which we held briefly within our four hands during the exchange, became the vehicle of those understood and unsaid peace offerings. A neighbour on the other side of the street witnessed the act with impassive phlegm, sitting on his summer aluminium floral folding chair listening to the radio news, passing an excited wooden toothpick from one corner of his mouth to the other.

"I'm going away, back to Bilbao."

"Will you contact...your daughter?"

"If I were allowed to..."

"Do you have an address to give us?"

"Rosa has all the pertinent details"- thus severing my prior monopoly of his life.

"Did you really marry my sister?"

"Yes, of course!" said Nacho decently.

"Is she unwell?" I said, prolonging the parting.

"She imagines things..."

"Are they true, Nacho?" I had all the rights to that question.

"Some of them will always be true," Nacho said with his voice in a quiver. "All I meant was to set you free, and to love her."

"And you have."

Our next-door neighbour to the left, opened his door to begin the summer evening preparations on his stepped portion of pavement, with chair, radio, cigarette and bellowing to his wife for her to join him.

"Goodbye Celia," and he disappeared downhill, out of our lives, puzzling the toothpicking neighbour, who could not believe his good luck as a spectator of an unfolding drama.

"Is Rosa back then?" He rocked himself in the un-rocking chair.

"Yes, she is not well," I managed to utter under the

circumstances, holding a three-month old baby in my arms, deposited there by the man all around town knew had been courting me the year before.

"Hope she gets better!"

"Me too, give her our regards," the other next-door neighbour interjected before I thanked all of them around and went indoors with my foster cargo filling my empty hands, my heart and life perfectly complete from that moment on.

"And that is how you came to be Ana. Deplorable but fortuitous; which other way would your mother and I have been granted a daughter?"

"Why didn't you tell me this before, Tita?"

"Your mother would not hear of it. She made me promise that I would never divulge her ignominy, especially to you."

I closed my eyes and I repeated to myself "tell my daughter that I love her" expecting some terrible yearning, a discovered loss, the emptiness of orphanhood but there were no reverberations around my childhood memories because they seemed happy. Collected scenes rushed past me and nothing was missing in my concept of childhood wellbeing. I had not had a father but instead I had had a loving aunt and a protective chocolate-cake-baking grandmother.

Then I remembered my daughter Aurora.

"Why are you telling me this now?"

"What retribution can I expect to be added to my eternal damnation?"

"Oh, come on now, Tita, tell me why?"

Two yellow Mediterranean scorpions, the last two, struggled

on the tallest branch of the oleander bush, finally lost their grip, and landed over the carcasses of their fellow-creatures, producing crackling noises muffled in their own dust. The vegetable cadaver that my oleander bush was, began to change colour from the root up, and it came alive gradually. Our autumn corner was not so sodden any more. A dry breeze descended from the hills above dragging the scorpion debris out of the flowerbed, across the grass and through the open gate in a cloud of yellow dust and crushed shells.

Ed was asleep in his chair, wrapped in his blanket, though he told me later that he was fully aware of the conversation taking place before him somehow. The doctor had warned us of the last symptoms of his deterioration; his debilitating efforts to keep awake, constant fatigue and false sleep until his last siesta might come. He would not be in pain. He would lose all lower mobility, then he would become incontinent. Not possible to say how long he had, months, weeks, or days. It all depended on his fortitude…or could be my entreating, telling him stories without an end, like a Scheherazade.

I beckoned him gently to wake up, but I instantly forgot him when my auntie intervened.

"He has only a few days, Ana," she prophesied, straightening her body. I turned around in dismay to see if Ed had heard her and back again to her "How can you say that?" I asked in a whisper, getting up myself.

"I just know."

"What else do you know?" I begged avidly, convinced of her clairvoyant powers from beyond our world and recalling her former honesty. She glanced at Ed, then through the open gate to the sea below, with calculating demeanour, but this evening it was tamed and glowing, with liquid reflections of a violet tint.

"Ed is a good man."

Then, I thought of poor Ed, Ed alone without a family of his own to mourn his passing. The man who married a stranger native of the country he had chosen to retire to, to find a self-exiled wife instead. Ed who had loved me from afar. The man, who came back from Spain moribund, his love prevailing over his illness until the day that I might return the compliment. Peace would be with him even before his death, in as big a dose as it would be in my power to administer, with a month's postponement of my work to make it happen, and my well-stocked larder of unused love at his disposal. "I know that your daughter still thinks of you Ana."

And then, I remembered my daughter. "Tell me, Tita, did my father ever pay me a clandestine visit?" Tita still hesitated, fidgeting with her hands, looking here and there while the afternoon faded with magenta light, contouring my aunt's shape like a russet aura.

"What about that very nice man we always encountered reading on that zoo bench, when I used to take you to the summer shoe fair in Valencia and we had lunch together, potato omelette sandwiches, under the acacia tree?"

"That very nice man who always bought us eucalyptus sweets and I had to keep it a secret because girls were not supposed to take sweets from strangers?"

"He was no stranger Ana; he was your father".

"And there I was thinking all those years imagining that you and he might have been…"

"So we were, in our own kind of way."

"Out of my sepia memories the images came, sitting on the bench, not too close to call the attention of the passers-by, not too far apart as to make the conversation a mere protocol. He was offering me sweets, which I kept for the train journey, and Tita Celia was unwrapping the sandwiches and offering him half of hers 'have some of it, it's much too big for me', and him replying 'if you don't mind, thank you', and Tita would say 'this is Ana my niece, Ana, come for your sandwich'… 'such a lovable child, does she do well in school?'…'she's very clever'. My first recollections of our very nice man are neutral, however as time advanced, I became aware of the punctuality of those annual chance encounters with our bench-sharer, and I invested them with romantic overtones."

"Did you have contact with him, Tita?"

"Oh, no, no, no. There was never any contrivance about our meetings, only blind faith in our common destiny. It was my duty as a manager of the shoe-shop to visit the fair every September and it was cheaper to have lunch on one of the zoo benches, and more becoming of a single woman on her own, than a café-bar. We met during my third trip on that very bench, each of us with a companion, and we exchanged courtesies, giving our reasons for being in the city, and parted company with a handshake. The following year I asked your mother's permission to take you with me and she, finding no moral obstacle in my offer, which also granted her a few days of unhindered piety, caretaking at the vicarage without you tugging along, consented. I took you then unsure of the outcome. At lunchtime we left the fair and got the electric tram to the zoo, and the same for three days. On the fourth day of the fair on the same numbered tram at the same time and on the same bench, he was there sitting and reading the paper. I terminated the visit while it was still proper to remain next to each other as in-laws and appearing inconsequential to you Ana, "we must go now if we want to get the 4.30'..."I'll bid you goodbye then." "Come on Ana and say goodbye to this nice man". We met once a year, on the same bench during the next ten years but suddenly you lost interest in the shoe-fair trip. You outgrew the inertia of the zoo bench where life had stopped happening and were fascinated by more interesting things like the neighbour's son, your maths teacher, and your horoscope. That incalculable source of excitement defeated our common destiny, your father's, and mine, and left us drifting…"

"Didn't you meet again?"

"Once, I arrived at our private bench to cancel our meetings, and to give him a picture of you, and he gave me the key to the house he had bought in Valencia. It was in your name, and he took me to see it from the outside, and after he accompanied me to get the 4.30 train back home. That was the last time I saw him. The last time."

"If we had kept in touch, he would have known of your wedding. He would have discovered the identity of your husband. He would have warned me of the unsuitability of his house as a safe haven where I took your daughter. If he had been the killer of your mother, Ana, he would be alive today, because he would have planted the bomb, and he would have made a fast escape to the frontier, as they all did. The day of the bus bombing he had come from Bilbao to Valencia, to sit on the zoo bench, as he did every year. He was just a Basque drifting alone without his common destiny, waiting to see his daughter one more time. The wrong Basque caught in the General's war."

"You cannot live under that terrible burden, Tita."

"I am not alive, Ana," Tita Celia retorted in retreat, following the downhill breeze toward the sea, enveloped in that evening russet aura, and exiting the garden through the open gate.

14 AN EPIC JOURNEY

"We had to prepare for the worst in the next few days", the oncologist, Dr Patterson, had revealed to us during our appointment the day before. Ed awoke next morning unable to feel both legs, soaked in his own urine, alarmed, and confused. He "could not call pain to that nagging discomfort he felt", he said, trying to comfort me. His advancing death was exhausting his vitality and yet "it was not that too often whispered and dreaded cancer pain to warrant all my fussing and the doctor's visits," he insisted, waving his right hand dismissively, his only mobile extremity at his service.

My impotence was maddening.

I dared not be still or quiet in his presence for fear of hearing that deadly beast eating its way through his spine to his heart. A mythic black crab tearing through bone and tissue relentlessly, leaving a blacker trail of baby crabs to feed on the body of the man I was beginning to love.

I hovered around him to make sure that he was comfortably installed while he observed all my movements. I spied on him for signs. Do not ask what signs or signs of what, because I did not know it myself.

Ana and her messenger birds

The guilt he experienced for his painless canker was a hurtful spectacle, so obvious he was in his efforts of expiation, so compliant, so self-effacing, that I felt unworthy of my own existence. My tribulations and heartaches shrank to mere disappointments in comparison to his dwindling life, and with his knowledge of it. The grave events which had brought me to the British shores and had prompted my past and recent actions had shifted position, lost importance besides the enormity of his impending fate. My grievances were not terminal; moreover, they were circumstantial, the result of an odd situation that colluded with a crucial epoch in which it happened and the convenient mix of people to set it apart from minor upsets.

And circumstances change, incessantly.

The marine view was majestic. Ed had fallen asleep again. Lunchtime careered through the bay window unused, ignored, and sunny, mortifyingly good-weathered. Loud noises were heard at the back of the house. The incessant clonk, clonk of rolling stones could be distinguished between the regular chatter of nature. It was an imperious call, the call of my dead and one I did obey; not without throwing a last glance at Ed, but he continued to sleep. I trod carefully downstairs avoiding the creaking points. "They" were already visible through the conservatory windows, the black shape digging at the far left corner of the garden, and the white smaller figurine, with her feet immersed in water pushing ostrich-egg-shaped pebbles to the edge of the flooded hole, building a neat dike to contain the rising water, in which she existed.

Ana and her messenger birds

I crossed my new garden, and sat on a mossy tree-stump by their side. The winter malaise that had attacked that corner, was also greening the white-laced hem of my unknown teenaged aunt and namesake's dress, matching the rancid green mantle creeping about the ground amongst soil and stones, up the cornered fence and everywhere in that side of the garden. Even the fog hovering at ground level in parts, had a greenish tinge of malevolent presage. My grandmother Carolina was persistent in her digging efforts, like a convict on hard labour, and likewise her task had no visible meaning or end, not to me that is, dredging the southern edge of the flooded hole, for it to house the ever-rising level of water. She must have perforated the walls of the subterranean stream feeding the hill above us.

My goose-pimpled body resented that unhealthy spectacle spread thereon, whereas my soul feared it instinctively… poor Ed.

A shallow flooded grave.

Was it occupied or in waiting? I wondered. Without remission they toiled, in an ominous steely silence so oppressive that its morbid weight was pushing inwards the incipient spring which dared to intrude into that gelid corner, while the rest of the garden and the south of England enjoyed mild weather, benign to people and propitious to plants. Clonk, clonk, clickety-clonk, the pebbles cried on being dragged along the edges of the pond.

"What are you doing, Ana?" I asked the child-form.

"I believe she's lining the bottom of the river with them," my grandmother answered me instead.

"Have you spoken with her?" I queried with bewilderment.

"Oh, no, dear me! She inhabits the limbo of the infants, far away from my world of pain and memories."

"Why does she do it, then?"

"It must be an innate reflex picked up on the river-bed in Guernica."

"Stop her, please, stop digging that hole or she will drown in it."

"But it can't be stopped, or I shall never find all my daughters. I must persevere if all my daughters have to meet me in death."

"Why in the water? Why in this cold weather when spring is here all around us?"

"Winter lives in my heart dear, and the whys and becauses…I ignore. One day, tired of searching the infinite, I felt like digging this spot in your garden. Little I knew of the spring running under it, and less I suspected of the attraction the water held for my oldest daughter; so, I will dig in earnest, as if my life depended on it. Like you breathe or the earth rotates. I can't stop until we all rest in peace; this I know."

"And when will you rest in peace, grandma?"

"Who knows?" she sighed and sat on the pile of earth she had just produced, which already frozen, hard and frost-powdered, having the appearance of a lunar rock formation.

"In my late life, you know, I used to think that death would provide a rest in peace to all, a stop to all life and its side effects. I had even wished it would come to visit me more than once, to take me where angels dwell but the slight thought of my orphaned girls always did the trick but …

In this vast abyss of deadness,

Where are my promised angels?

Where lies that kingdom of heaven,

For us to meet at last?"

The ground moss began its ascension through her black skirts. Her angry prayers had fuelled the pernicious green in its upward march. Her anger created a cold breeze. The back gate blew open with a lugubrious crying of rusty hinges. A tall figure came through it ignoring the pleasures of my four seasons' garden and approached our trio. Grandmother and I were mesmerised because my mother did not look a day older than I did. She walked delicately over the rough ground dressed in her favourite blue colour. Her porcelain face and demure demeanour denounced her life-long and death-longer beatific delusion. She hovered around counting a wooden rosary unaware of our presence, inhabiting the same limbo her younger sister Ana gravitated on. She was at peace. A stranger to me in death as she had been in life.

Grandmother understood the reality though the improbable communication between the three did not diminish their reunification.

"If I could be permitted to see Celia!" Grandma begged me.

"I don't know how to help you Yaya," I pleaded.

"People are very resourceful in extreme circumstances," was her invitation.

"What extreme circumstances?" I asked hoping that that was the right leading question.

"Situations of imminent disaster…"

"I was never successful against those," I regretted aloud.

"Your daughter is a fine woman today…"

"Because of me?"

"Well, it isn't because of the devil of her father, believe me."

"Why should I believe the exoneration I desperately want to hear?"

"Sacrifices deserve recognition, not exoneration, Ana."

"And yours, Yaya?"

"Back in my day we didn't sacrifice, we survived."

"How did you survive?"

"Like any other mother on her own, who undertook the crossing of Spain in wartime, hiding my personal assets from the curious minds of every kind of man we encountered on our way south and east. Some soldiers wanted a bit of fun before the attacks or retreats; civilians demanded it among the chaos and ruins unless, that was, one happened to be amorphous…old…astute and indispensable to their diets.

Able cooks, makers of feeding miracles were in high demand by the opulent families who could afford the ingenuity of the women-confectioners of cakes without flour and that I became on the river-side south of Guernica, after the death of my poor Ana. There was no time to cry. Two daughters and fifty thousand Reales depended on me for safekeeping. The hundred or so of us women and children who survived the river-crossing, regrouped in small parties, inconspicuous to the passing troops and easier to feed from scavenging and we began our march south to the warmer regions of Valencia; where it was believed that the fruit trees remained laden with fruit at the roadsides of every town and village, with branches so heavy and low that small children could harvest them.

I had befriended a lonely woman in her fifties, or so her general appearance proclaimed, of frayed attire and leathered face...or she might have befriended me. Ours became a peculiar relationship: I should provide for her and give her the shelter of a family, while she would look out for me and care for my two daughters if one day I did not come back from work. A woman on her own had an inauspicious future. An old woman alone was easy prey to mortal illnesses. A young widowed mother on her own also was an abandoned treasure prone to be looted by any unsavoury character. However; a feminine group acquired respectable dimensions, becoming an impregnable fortress, where the prosperous alliance of the even forces of desperate women transcended the obduracy of war.

This woman, Amalia, was compliant to extravagance, not in the least servile to others (don't get me wrong), she was extremely grateful to those who mattered to her welfare, in an enduring and endearing way, solicitous without calculation, her generosity equalled only by the extreme care I took of her. I ate and slept always after Amalia, to make sure she never lacked her due comforts for her constant services. The trade of affection and social obligations is better accomplished between women, I must say, because as good as my late husband had been, (bless him), and he was not an unfair man, the general social transactions needed to the daily living were easier exchanged with another woman, than with your own husband.

Our unashamed familiarity procured us warmth in winter, food when it was scarce, safety among angry men and joy while all about us was death and constant attacks from one army or the other.

The first lesson Amalia taught me was that a woman, like a soldier, needed camouflage. Amalia introduced me to the art of uglifying, instant mummies of a civil war like living corpses existing on the verges of the very life in which we tried to survive... but it worked. With two shawls wrapped around my upper half to produce a hapless silhouette, Amalia showed me how to slow my pace to an unnoticeable flexing of my buttocks, to walk very old.

The morning after our river-crossing (God have Ana with him!), when the sun was but a blood-orange far away beyond the Valencian fields, and before the entire band of refugees would scatter over the south mountain-trails, my would-be companion began to teach me and the rapidly gathered crowd the secrets of that art of uglifying; which she had learnt in some theatrical circle in Bilbao, where she had worked as a personal dresser for a diva. She enacted the rituals and preparations she had seen performed and she repeated verses of an obscure poem to become inconspicuous, as she gradually changed her appearance, to the marvel of all around. She regaled our ears with a few elocution lessons to lower the pitch of the voices of young women and recited the three laws of preservation, she called them, swearing by them, alleging a long and virginal life spent unmolested and unnoticed by every man of any ilk and age.

Ana and her messenger birds

Do not avert your eye from the approaching man.

Never level eyes during a quiet interlude with a man.

Avoid being caught in furtive observations.

She was of the opinion that men being of an enticeable condition and women of an alluring nature, both sets could never meet without a chemical reaction. So her eye had never gone astray from its zealous socket, and there she was, approaching old age in one piece, as unnoticed as a pallid moon at midday. However naïve her arguments, they impelled the refugee congregation to contrive and contain their appearance and of that mind inclined for fear or persuasion. I am sure there were a few lives and virtues saved during our pilgrimage south, crossing rivers, valleys and mountains, to where most republicans were fleeing those days. Even the Republican government moved there for a year, escaping the nationalists.

I soon realised that my travelling companion was not what she seemed because once we were on our own, hidden from prying eyes, she used to unfold her physical dimensions, stretching her personality in an umbrella-like fashion for my daughters to bask under her protection.

Amalia made us laugh on our empty stomachs and tremble cold with fear in mid-August. Hers was not an industrious nature; her mind toiled by day with elaborate schemes to keep us safe, which I would make happen, and by night she recited and declaimed stories, anecdotes, pieces of old gossip, and popular myths spinning the yarn that kept her busy and well-loved.

During that year we spent travelling together, she fought for us the war we were always fleeing but never entirely avoiding. We managed to cross the warpath of every General in the area and survive on her wits and my hard labour and still at night we learnt to set aside our troubles to hear her stories.

Bad memories were stored away till better days arrived to deal with them. Heartaches and mortal longings were superbly exploited in her repertoire. Our exodus seemed a stroll compared to the fate of her Dumas heroes. Her Dickensian plots were more sinister than the appalling atrocities committed around us in the name of the country or God, or the Republic, or the Party. A young woman was de-breasted and killed within earshot from where we lodged in Vitoria, still in our Basque country. In Logroño, we witnessed two Nationalist executions, where Communist militiamen were undressed and gagged and shot in the back of their heads. In Calatayud I too…but never mind! A column of misplaced civilians was massacred in the pass of Escandón but we still survived under the command of Amalia, who told us to play dead amongst the bodies.

And we moved on southwards.

We kept moving on, cooking for hungry lieutenants, mayors, doctors, comrades, even one General; in fact I lent my culinary services to any group of men large enough to allow my regular scavenging to pass unnoticed, at the request of Amalia. She cast a benign spell on us 'to help us cope', she said the day we parted company, but we had not minded all her scheming and usurping of hearts, because that had been our bargain. Amalia was a wandering spirit encapsulated in a feeble body, born to die alone because of her fear of men, without a family of her own, fostering other men's families on her way south to God knows where. She never said what her destination was. She did continue onwards probably to the southernmost point of the country and once there, she might have turned her aspirations northward, in a migratory flight of fancy.

I did not know my destination either, though I constantly told my two remaining daughters that we were to meet their father in Valencia. But I knew I would recognise my destination at a glance, whether behind one battle-line or the other, it being an odd place or a charming one, prosperous or war-worn, the knowledge would come to me as a certainty as these things come.

When we arrived at the dilapidated, but still operational, staging post of Baños, after two days of rambling through the hills and countryside, I was promptly engaged as a cook for the local vet-cum-doctor. Mrs. Lola or Auntie Lola, as she was universally known, had been given special powers to enrol personnel for the best families in the town. By the privilege of her position as post-mistress turned publican and labour exchanger, she did so as quickly as the trains stopped by her establishment, and her voluminous humanity allowed her to approach the newcomers.

That staging-post called Las Ventas rested on a strategic point, one of the highest transiting mountain passes parallel to the Madrid-Valencia railway line, of which it was its occasional station. The Iberian mountain chain spread to the south, west, and north of it, in continuous ridges and fertile valleys. One mile to the east, the town was sprawling downhill facing the warm Mediterranean breeze with white-washed walls and its peripheral boundaries were dotted with industrial chimneys and arable red soil. A mediaeval fortress protruded over the rooftops of the lower half linking the separated two halves of the town by means of a stone bridge still standing and in use. The hillside underneath it had been carved by a prehistoric torrent now slithering between its rugged verges creating rapids and pools for swimming.

From our position, the river could be seen meandering under minor bridges collecting water from many rivulets and springs that sipped through the hillside, to gather the strength and volume that fed half a dozen paper mills along its valley-course within the Olla valley. A salty wind ascended from afar, from Valencia, from the sea. Whatever the outcome of our war, I thought Baños would be a prosperous place and with time it would attract a plentiful supply of decent men for my daughters. I envisaged a good future for my daughters. Baños was my destination.

I had found my Valencia.

Amalia instead had found, in the concourse with Mrs. Lola, her reason to move on further south: "the whole area was teeming with Reds, Anarchists, and Church-burners". In my opinion and after one year on the roads it was well founded, the entire country was full of thugs and opportunistic scavengers on both sides. We ourselves had scavenged also and lied and squatted, however ours was not political thuggery, it was a necessity, though Amalia had forgotten that we all were once good people and capable of reverting to what we once had been, when the conflict ended.

Ana and her messenger birds

I wanted to be in Baños when that time came, and she did not. To all my arguments she had a rebuke, also she felt the terrible presentiment (she whispered) that something worse was to come after the war. "The country will plunge into an abyss for a very long time" she elaborated with a fearful feverish stare never exposed before and she began her quivering fits from lips to voice to knees, as a caramel flan on the path of an earthquake.

A group of nuns approached us on foot, each one holding a travelling Gladstone bag and a rosary in their respective little white hands. They were catching the next train to the Valencian capital. They were making their way south to the warmer and more pious region of Andalucía, having exited Baños in fear of their lives and virtue. Mind you, God gave them enough sang-froid to gather all valuables in the convent and bury them, they expostulated without any physical gesture and a lot of celestial nomenclature.

Amalia pointed out to them the latent danger of a long journey undertaken by unaccompanied saint-women. They agreed on the need to find a chaperone wise in the mundane pitfalls of womanhood. My companion suggested an unusual route from Valencia onwards to the south. They in a chorus, graciously invited her to join them "that is if she was not otherwise engaged", they obligingly enquired of me with a unanimous tilting of their coiffeurs. I duly surrendered my companion alleging the end of my journey and they commended me and my daughters to their highest Saints.

Amalia had been silent during that brief transition. Being the object of such exchange between noble women and a needful mother had vindicated her value and lightened the burden of guilt.

God needed her now.

The train from Madrid whistled behind the immediate hill. The nuns counted another wooden bead, Amalia gave my daughters a sorrowful kiss, looked at me for the last time and went to join the departing flock of swallows in black and white gliding across the platform, disappearing amongst their flapping habits and bags filled with God's silver. My daughters were quietly sobbing but I could not reach out to console them, neither could I tell them how much I loved them because I was crying too, because we were alone for the first time, facing our uncertain future. Left alone all exposed to remember our heartaches, to miss Amalia, to miss the loved ones.

But I did love them.

But I could not tell them without betraying my poor Ana in the river.

But I did love them.

I would not have made it in later years without my Celia.

But I could never tell her.

At that precise moment, my Aunt Celia came through the open gate and ignoring her usual autumnal plot at the right of it, she neared us observing the familiar group through tearful eyes.

"I heard you calling me mother," she said, producing a handkerchief, which she handed to her tearful mother.

"If only you knew Celia," grandma half articulated between sobs and sniffles.

Ana and her messenger birds

"I know now mother," Aunt Celia answered, looking for another tree-stump to sit on. My mother ambled around the verges of the flooded hole, counting rosary beads, and little Ana had not yet finished her stonework. By then, I had become irrelevant to the scene. I had no way of conveying my love to those who were unaware of my presence. There was more of a material difference between our worlds. I felt a physical urge to touch them, to rub cheek against cheek, mixing our tears, to press my relatives against my bosom, and feel their old warmth, unlike them now that kept a polite distance, and spoke with monotone voices about tragic matters, such as their lives and deaths.

They became a pale reflection of their former selves. I began to fear their disintegration if I attempted to bridge the gap. Their unfinished business had kept them apart for too long, to be cut short now by my unnatural intervention. I left them in the wintry corner of my garden, enveloped in that malevolent low mist, and returned to Ed.

15 A MISSED APPOINTMENT

There are no certainties in life that time or experience have not discredited. We invent certainties to make life bearable. We have created them like points of reference from the beginning of time, and they are natural depictions of the human condition that promotes faiths where knowledge is lacking. Some believe in life after death, some in reincarnation, some in heaven but one certainty belies all embellishment; the only certainty of our condition which keeps our pride in check: death.

A peaceful death or tormented, painful, or painless, a sudden death or diagnosed one, a graceful demise or shameful passing, deceased or gone, the effect is the same to all alive: we cease to be to become dead. Ed's death had been diagnosed in the morning, foretold within a margin of hours, with signs to look for as if outdoing death at her own game could serve as consolation, but death came in unannounced. She caught us unawares, depriving us of the last farewell.

When I went upstairs with his dinner and half sat him on the bed, his life was still very much within him, even though he had to be fed his soup very slowly, and his eyes could not remain open for long, he had the stamina to maintain our conversation going. He wanted to know whether I had seen my Aunt Celia again, and I reported to him the developments in the garden that afternoon. He finished his soup, and I began to spoon out the yoghurt, when he opened his eyes and said: "Can you hear?" but I could not hear anything.

"Are you expecting anybody?" He insisted

"No…"

"The doorbell…?"

"I'm afraid not, I never saw the need to fit it…with you gone and me working from home…you know I detest doorbells."

"There is someone calling…" Ed was adamant.

"I will see who it is" and I went downstairs to the front door where an absolute calm prevailed. I opened it and looked around in vain. Nothing. Ed must have misplaced the noise; for which I went instead to the conservatory and to my astonishment I saw my dead relatives advancing toward me across the patio. I did not know their intentions, but I assumed they were coming in. I waited for them in the belief that they could cross walls and conservatory glass doors if they wanted to, but they stopped at the door very quietly. Finding their inaction across our glass partition puzzling, I did the polite thing and most rational to living people: I opened the door and let them in. They came in one-by-one, grandma, Ana, mother and Tita Celia overlooking my presence and they made their silent way to the foot of the stairs. There they stopped hovering at ground level.

Ana and her messenger birds

A sudden recognition came to me with the weight of a tombstone, cold and lonesome, and the dreadful thought propelled me upstairs, but they began the ascent before me. As I ran, a spray of words flashed across my eyes like the credits at the end of a film.

Signs, misread, someone calling, signs, expecting someone.

Of course, we were, we had been expecting it all along!

Oh dear, what if he had been afraid?

If he had had last requests?

He had died alone!

He had died!

Died…alone!

His eyes were closed, his hands cold and inert under the breakfast tray. I retrieved his unfinished dinner and nestled his body in my arms… but his warmth was fast escaping to unknown regions, far away from me, from our recent kisses, far from his love confession, abandoning our conversations and forsaking me.

Often, we had discussed the certainty of death and his in particular, to prepare me for when it came, overlooking the fact of his own absence once dead. My dead relatives were hovering at the foot of the bed, mesmerised by some invisible miracle bemusing to them. I turned to them with reproach.

"Couldn't you have let me know in time?"

"Death always comes alone, even when unexpectedly dearest", murmured grandma.

"But where is he now if not with you?" I cried, holding Ed in the cradle of my arms, rocking him to and fro.

Ana and her messenger birds

"He is at peace," said Aunt Celia after a long consultation amongst them. "At peace now and forever" added grandmother and their contours began to soften against the wardrobe, appearing less solid, like reflected images on a pool of rippling waters. One by one and in the same order again, they went downstairs and disappeared from my life.

"At peace now and forever."

So easy to deceive is the man who has beliefs, whose faith has never been tainted by the life that produces it. Love is what he had needed, the certainty of my love and I had not given it in a clear way. That conviction that we would travel eternity together. The certainty before the parting that all had not been in vain. The man whom I was beginning to love like love should happen, had died in peace, my dead had said, reclined upon certainties of which I was not certain, nor proud of having caused them, and neither sure of doing it. The guessing game we had started during his illness had been abandoned for lack of living players. Did it really matter who I had been, or was the price of my search, who I had become? I wished I could be deceived as easily into peace as the person who has faith.

I looked around the room, and it looked bigger now. I turned to the bedside table to call the doctor, but I noticed that its drawer and the lamp were on the floor, as well as the telephone; first, I repositioned the telephone and called the surgery to ask our doctor to come, then I began to collect the contents of the drawer strewn about that side of the bed, some photographs of happier days, two passports, and a weighty envelope amongst a myriad of personal nick-nacks.

Ana and her messenger birds

Ed must have tried to open it with his only able hand and had pulled too hard. This must have been his last thought and action. I put everything back hurriedly except the envelope, which seemed uncharacteristically large for the drawer. I turned it around in my hands, and there was Ed's handwriting, addressed to me.

Dearest Ana,

Only, and only open this envelope, when you are at peace with yourself.

I sat there, on the floor, with the envelope in my hands until the doctor came. My hands so much like my aunts, I thought, would never feel empty again, because he had loved those hands; he had loved them during our brief marriage, in the distance during his voluntary exile, and during his illness. He had loved my secrets, my silences and my confessions. I had finally had the love of a good man and from that certainty I drew a new strength, a new sense of identity to defy what was to come.

I was not an image of myself, I was not
a pale reflection of my good intentions.
I was not the product of my own emotions.
The opinion of myself I was not,
because I was just what I was.
What I always suspected myself to be;
I was all my life's recollections,
the reason of what defeats me,
my own hell and consecration.
Because I was what I was.
And I could not help but being

Ana and her messenger birds

the unwilling prey of a rapacious man,
the reason why Grandma baked,
my aunt's beloved ward…
and my mother's insanity.
The memories of my dead I was,
…but not the mother I was meant to be.
I was not at peace indeed.

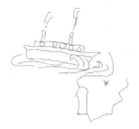

16 THE VOYAGE

I had anticipated sublime emotions befitting the circumstance: the quickening of the heart, an overpowering ancestral recognition… but what I experienced on setting foot in Bilbao, was just that vague satisfaction of the traveller seeing the first signs of her destination; for I was plagued by a sense of foreboding, contracted on board the ship, and no earthly pleasures could alleviate it.

During the three-day voyage from Portsmouth I had been preoccupied as to what lay ahead, in my prodigal return. Since I had taken that final step, after Ed's funeral, and I had arrived at too long overdue decisions, believing my ghosts exorcised, I thought I had set the past to rest; however, I had seen my harbingers again, not once or twice but constantly and openly marauding about the ferry.

Yes, I was not mistaken or momentarily confused.

They were travelling in a conspicuous group of four on deck, at times occupying the empty deckchairs or promenading aimlessly. They would materialise unceremoniously startling me and would pass me without a glance, never seeking me…and I did not approach them fearing nefarious consequences for them if I did.

During their walkabouts at dusk, with the angled light profiling them, they would become nearly translucent if caught unawares, then they would reach for the railings of the top deck of the boat; which for some unexplained coincidence were eerily avoided by all on board, and there spent the evenings and nights staring at the horizon, letting the sea breeze play with their hair and dresses, as if they were flags, turning more diaphanous the nearer we sailed to the Spanish Basque coast, braving the cold winds and tall waves that rocked the sides of the ferry as we entered the Bay of Biscay. Thus, they kept vigil undeterred by the weather conditions, like protective ship figureheads at the bow of old ships.

Since the death of Ed ten days before, they had not visited my garden. I had waited and waited for their return seated on the edge of his deathbed, like inanimate objects do in empty houses, one day…two…three.

The fourth brought my coma to a natural end.

The fifth came and my ex-husband was definitely resting in peace.

On the morning of the seventh I was ready to bury the man whom I had just begun to love, without fuss, only a friend or two of mine, some mutual acquaintances from the days of our marriage and ourselves. Not a great social accumulation to justify his fifty years. His restless travelling had not procured him close friends, and life had given him no relatives either. But something happened on the left corner of my garden during the funeral. Dead or living hands could not have humanly brought about the change. It was that natural metamorphosis of winter into spring conscribed within the duration of a funeral service that made it memorable: the dreaded flooded grave became a serene pond fully lined with smooth river boulders, inhabited by frogs and newts, and water lilies, having the feel of an established natural pool. The moss, which during the past month had corrupted the area, had given way to grasses of all colours and sizes. Ed would have liked it, I remember thinking. I remember thinking of my daughter Aurora too, with the urgency of a condemned prisoner after being given a pardon, conjuring the picture of a young Tita Celia in my mind because I had no clues other than the familiar likeness throughout our generations.

I longed to hear her womanly voice, her story.

I had been granted a three weeks extension on my translation deadline after a few phone calls and some badly concocted explanation, which was clearly not fully believed but, as I was one of their most reliable translators, they graciously conceded. I had procrastinated fifteen years to confront the fear that had plagued me for too long, but I felt that my harbingers' return augured more than Ed's passing. Thus troubled, I stepped onto my forebears' land. A land full of traffic signs in Euskera, not in Spanish, in a taxi that rushed me through a labyrinthine route of secondary streets, giving me an unauthorised tour of the city; a Gothic church, the iron railings of a Convent, the Town Hall Square, whole streets where all balconies had the regional flag wrapped around the railings, then the outskirts of Bilbao, the tortuous road to Guernica, to which he charged me accordingly addressing me in Euskera, which I could not reciprocate.

But I had not travelled alone…the five of us alighted in silence, in the main square of Guernica. I paid the exorbitant fare and headed the ghostly group to the cemetery. I had to find the whereabouts of my grandfather's grave, far beyond logical reasoning, urged by emotional forces, my feet moved on impulse through the streets, asking for directions to passers-by. The afternoon was dripping from every cornice and window-ledge. The vertical neon lights offered their wet messages undefeated by the damp: pension, hostel, pharmacy, and so on in the vanishing afternoon, flickering beacons to the lost visitor in two languages. Recent rains had not yet dried under the weakest sun ever to hang on an April evening. I scoured the late shopping crowds now and then, to ascertain if my dead companions kept pace with me, walking in pairs as they were. I slowed my pace to walk closely behind them, convinced as I was, that they would eventually take me to their destination. We left the centre veering consistently to the right and the left, leaving the more popular shops and day-trippers behind, exiting the residential quarters and crossing the less well lit streets, in the direction of the tall line of cypresses that peered through the high walls at the top of the brow of the nearest hill; which could be seen from every street perpendicular to it. My relatives seemed attracted to those sentinels of the dead, and their ascetic forms were the key to their meandering I thought, climbing the shallow hill that separated them from us.

Ana and her messenger birds

The cemetery gates moaned with reticence at being opened. We all stopped in the central corridor of niches. They had difficulty following the trail between the scent of the omnipresent chrysanthemums, and the fresh cement used by the lapidarian to seal recent niches, still drying. They moved in the direction of the old part, then, grandmother stepped forward, chose a mortuary wall, and began to inspect the individual headstones of each niche and then… I knew. I knew that as dead as they were, as unlikely as it was of me ever to have guessed his whereabouts on my own, and as incredible as the visitations and concerns of my dead might look to others, with the same certainty, I knew that my missing grandfather (never found for sixty years) must be buried there, far from where he was killed, but in his Guernica, without a name, with many other unnamed graves. Far from his wife.

One by one we all joined in the search of the high walled corridors: dear daughters in pink granite, beloved husbands in black marble, forever missed children in gilded letters…grandma was showing signs of despair in translucent bouts. I asked a mourner by a recent stone, whether there was an older section or a war memorial, to which she indicated the enclosure beyond the mausoleum, tucked away, excused and forgotten. And there was a flat gravelled area, on the left corner of the cemetery walls. In its centre and circled by low posts with chains grew an oblong miniature meadow replete with uncut grass and wildflowers. A monumental panel had been erected beside the communal grave, displaying scores of names and photographs when available. Grandmother crossed the low chains and paced her black figure in circles, in the way that cats have of preparing their sleeping patch before lying down. When she found the right spot, she turned to us for the last time and slowly disappeared into the evening air, without preamble.

Tita Celia did not appear concerned by her sudden departure. She turned around and took charge of her two sisters with extreme care not to rob them of their eternal limbo. With delicate fingers she held their inanimate hands and the three went away through the same route as before. They glided more than walked over the empty streets. But I took a different route because there was something I had to buy before my departure. Until our separation, there had been a tacit understanding between us, my dead and me, whereas I had followed where they led, and listened when they spoke. It had been an unbalanced relationship. They knew I was seeking the memories I lacked. They had been in possession of my family history and they knew what lay on the other side of life and each of them wanted something before their night befell them. For myself ...I had seen through their eyes and heard through their ears during our past month together and peeped at the secrets of their pasts and beyond but now I wanted something as well, and I knew what lay on this side of life, what to expect.

And I wanted my life back. That life my Aunt died protecting, the life for which my mother lost her sanity. That other life nursed with infinite chocolate cakes from my grandmother's bosom.

"Oh Ed, Ed with a patient and loyal heart, who had loved me

in the dark before knowing me and before I knew my own heart. What might have you made of my errand?"

But...

It no longer mattered. I was intent on buying a defensive weapon to confront the past, to find Aurora, but I had to settle for a kitchen-knife from the only shop that I found open. With it in my handbag I returned to my waiting train to Logroño, armed with it and some courage.

My journey across the northern regions of Spain happened during the night, in deep sleep rocked into numbness by the motion of the train: the brain, shaken and scrambled, rested on a strange pillow devoid of its own pulse. I missed the departure of Little Ana somewhere between Guenrica and Durango, most probably during a bridge crossing along the river Nervión that had been her grave. I had not known her, nor known of her existence before Ed came home to die, but somehow she had become an intrinsic part of myself because Little Ana's drowning weighed on the consciousness of my family and that tragedy had set in motion a chain of events; which were still affecting my own daughter.

My namesake had come back to the liquid limbo where she belonged but my mother and Aunt did survive the nocturnal journey keeping vigil at the foot of my tiny bed, while the train crossed Castilla, during the short stop in Madrid and in the second train through the width of the quixotic region of La Mancha.

The restaurant coach was animated the following morning at breakfast time, with a sense of expectancy felt by all travellers. The rolling countryside yawned from house to house; miles of still wintering soil, of empty fields of wheat, and of naked vineyards later on, changing colour under the appearing and disappearing morning sun, distinctively delineating provincial borders by the way the colour of the land reacted to the light. If my geography teacher had not lied, we were more numerous in that coach than the sum of inhabitants per square kilometre we had covered, in the region we were crossing. The long stretches of flat land created very wide skies and long views.

Inside the restaurant, the aroma of coffee awoke the last vestiges of late dreams, the waiter glided through the moving carriage with diligence…and my remaining dead relatives appeared to be waiting to be served on the table by the bar. A humming chorus of conversation arose with that aroma. I had forgotten how much we loved to talk and the high volume in which our national pastime of over the table conversation is practised. We seem to be born with powerful larynxes and enduring eardrums. To my fellow passengers it was paramount to obscure the monotonous choo-choo-choo of the train, as if to compensate for the inaction of the landscape. The resonance of the life extracts of strangers spiced my breakfast, lengthening it unashamedly while their lives unfolded with candid ease around me, making me a part of their shared plots. All the players in our moving stage were aware of each other and were relishing the lack of intimacy. It was not an aberration grown out of our past captive society, but that Spanish virtue by which society thickens and gains consistency and flavour, leaving to the world of shadows and the intimacy only bed activities.

Ana and her messenger birds

To the old couple on the first table near the front connecting door, and dipping croissants in minute cups of coffee, the prices on board were an absolute robbery that would never have been allowed in their good old days. Thanks to God and their generous daughter who paid for their ticket, they could afford such a waste of good money "scandalous, scandalous" they echoed each other, and ate another dripping croissant leg, sending a myriad of gold sparkles with each movement of the woman's wrist, as she did so. Every bone of theirs had been patiently and joyously covered with flesh, giving them a childish appearance. Small as they were and immaculately dressed in a bygone fashion and dark clothes, and displays of solid gold accessories, they moaned their way through the breakfast of endless coffee, turning it bitter, as if to diminish the pleasure of their contented living.

In comparison, two commercial representatives, because nobody wears a suite like a sales rep, discussed the football results like expert television commentators, as they sipped black coffee, smoked American imported, and surveyed the voluptuous truffle-cake eating techniques of two precocious teenage girls on the next table, offering to pay for their breakfast as they paid for theirs. May was the month for commercial provincial fairs, bringing the otherwise unobtrusive army of salesmen out of the woodwork and into long distance trains and enduring Seat and Ford cars. They loved life, their life and their coffee breaks and spinning yarns about their travels.

The teenagers dressed in clothes two sizes smaller than

themselves, were performing their cake-eating technique for the benefit of the waiter, who in turn was bent on pleasing my smallest culinary whims, after assessing his better chance of being tipped. He hovered about the minuscule restaurant with the agility of a lizard and kept the two teenagers mesmerised and myself well-tended to, the two representatives perplexed about his undeserved good-luck and the old couple blissfully cosy, flicking from table to table like a bee. He made our journey more interesting answering questions of all kinds: yes he was from Madrid, yes there was a mid-morning coffee and snacks service, no the Valencian mountains were not part of the Pyrenees, yes prices were higher on the coast and no, he was not married but he had a long-standing boyfriend.

My mother and aunt looked on unperturbed by the obvious social changes, when in former times one would have cried with excitement and the other with indignation.

The countryside finally awoke. The wine province came and went. Olive and carob trees replaced the vines and scattered oaks in a landscape that grew tall with the advancing morning until the contours became familiar to me. We rolled in parallel with the Iberian mountain chain for a while, skirting the major peaks and valleys, constantly moving south, like a snake, looking for an exit to the Mediterranean. Soon we would cut across the mountain passes leading to the high Vegas of Valencia and to the historic staging post cum station of Baños.

There was water in abundance in the land of my childhood from underground springs and fountains, canals, rivers, and dams. The moisture rose from the depths of the subsoil perfuming every aspect of life. It carved every portion of her red soil, exuding that characteristic odour of fertile land: like a chocolate cake my grandmother used to say when describing her adopted country.

17 A STEPPING STONE

To leave the safety of my sleeper compartment was the most difficult decision I have ever taken, and I struggled to physically get up, walk to the waiting open door and step out in the space of thirty seconds. The funambulist suffers vertigo on the brink of his rope crossing, but he knows there is safety on the other side where that rope finishes, whereas I harboured little hope on the outcome of my errand. People do not really change with age, traits become more, or less pronounced though not different. Pasts cannot be shed like old skins at the point of transmutation to allow a different animal to emerge. Characters either soften or fray around the edges, but the essence of our being is the reason for our being. People (and Antonio in particular) might act in the same way repeatedly…if all circumstances could converge again.

Fear, that paralysing fear.

That debilitating illness that sips courage out of our lives.

I harboured little hope.

Once I were to set foot on common ground to Antonio and

myself, I would lose the anonymity that had shielded my recent bout of courage. It was so tempting to ignore the open door, to overlook the swinging placard that read "Las Ventas" and to carry on my railway journey to its natural end in Valencia, flanked by my two chaperones and to see their grand disappearing act into eternity: first my mother, I was sure on the road to Valencia, and last my aunt I guess in the apartment of my father; the house where she unsuccessfully hid my daughter and where she left her heart, but… stepped out I did, with borrowed courage, and a kitchen knife and Ed's envelope in my handbag, still unopened.

And the advanced May morning received me warmly, as if she had awaited my arrival since time immemorial dressed for it. The morning air and sounds and imagery were those of yesteryear when I knew them all with entitled familiarity. I had never left. The morning had never noticed my absence. The contorted pine trees perched over the railway remembered me. The giant agaves sprouted along the verges of the meandering road into Baños recognised me, and the birds…well, they sang as enthusiastically as ever. My aunt and mother were no longer with me because they had continued their epic journey east out of my life, without farewells and no last-minute glances, but I just caught their vanishing faces through the windows of the moving train.

There I was! They had delivered me to my destiny, my two mothers.

It was my mission to make it happen. How could I discover certain things without being discovered by certain people? If I remembered well the old staging-post, "Tía Encarna" was a well of information, and it may be quiet at that time of the morning, because the new motorway had reduced the traffic through the old National road to a steady local trickle, less sophisticated but richer in personal details.

The post was at the back of the station or the station at the back of the staging post; in reality the building had too solid fronts sandwiched between the railway and the National road. The door on the National road façade was open. I parted the timeless curtain of macaroni beads and went inside. It took a few seconds to get accustomed to much darker environs, and a lot more time to register the miscellany of services offered within. I had long forgotten the social magnitude of that unobtrusive establishment for the locals, the seasonal community, and the occasional passer-by. It seemed to have survived modernity and prosperity with hidden powers of its own. A few tables and chairs under the windows for the respectful eater, a vintage bar for the idle conversationalist, a small black board shouting "Today, paella", and a bigger one that hung replete with signed petitions, orders and reminders, which its enduring clientele was obliged to use in the absence of human attendance, happening very often.

I advanced further and was attracted by the tenuous light deep inside. Its source was the reigning seat of the old owner years ago, behind the second window. I reached the sepia-tinted corner, avoiding the empty butane gas bottles for the weekly collection of the scattered neighbourhood, side-stepping baskets of vegetables on sale and ignoring the inquisitive stare of three suspicious felines of obscure pedigree basking under the timid light that had discoloured the superfluous ping-pong table. And there she was, the owner's daughter-in-law as I last saw her some fifteen years back, with a negligible shift of position at the table. She was now occupying the owner's chair. Her resemblance with the by-gone mother-in-law did not stop at the occupational place, no; she had adopted the knitting habits of her obvious mentor. Her eyes never touched the garment she was producing but wandered continuously from her publican domain to the window, as if waiting for something to happen out there. She had also inherited the owner's wardrobe and wore it with the same propriety. Her figure had in the process expanded to fit the old woman's great humanity. Sometimes, accommodating daughters-in-law developed a better likeness than the mere family air of the son. She scrutinised my advance with a keen eye, appraising every detail of my anatomy and foreign attire, forgetting the window but did not fool me into thinking myself special because she honoured everybody with identical treatment and privilege.

I doubted whether she recognised me; moreover, I intended to maintain anonymity during my stay in Baños, and to keep my enquiries as fortuitous exchanges or small talk. She passed her index finger over the passive needle and adjusted it better between her overflowing right breast and her arm.

"Let my dead confound me if you are not poor Celia from the north!"

"No, I am not", I uttered with dismay seeing my plot aborted on the first manoeuvre.

"You must be then, her daughter Ana?" She said timidly not

for a faulty memory but for the exquisite pleasure of gossip.

"I am her niece", I had to admit before she extracted further information.

"Of course, you are! And are we here for a long stay or en-route?"

"I don't know at this stage…it's a personal matter."

"Oh, I see…are we visiting old acquaintances, seeing old faces?"

"Sort of", I gave up the pretence. We knew who the tacit subject of our exchange was, but his identification was not required; in case some prospective customers might scoop her news broadcast or my surprise visit.

"As my mother-in-law used to say 'hard weeds die hard.'"

"Not before their time", I embroidered upon her riddle to confirm our mutual interest, thus starting the enquiry proper, but being more curious than tactful, she prevaricated on matters that were of the public domain, though still relevant to our conversation, to establish intimacy.

"Is your girl doing all right? Not that I like to pry on the misfortunes of others. As you must know, we were all shocked and outraged at the time and concerned about you, left alone in such conditions…and with no-one to turn to…but 'it is a fact', my mother-in-law would say, that tragedies come in threes, and it is true that every dog has its day…and you deserve yours, child", she went on with hearty eagerness, so unexpected for its late coming fifteen years on. I was drawn to her for still remembering me and mine with clarity and sympathy, and I felt compelled to confidences. "I have to settle a delicate matter with him, to make sure it is safe for me and my daughter to meet. Do you know of his whereabouts nowadays?"

"Well…him being a local celebrity, of the notorious kind I mean, his comings and goings are of everyone's interest. Why, only yesterday my Tomas and myself were commenting on his sudden retirement."

"Has he retired from politics?"

"From politics, public life, and life altogether I would say. Word came up from Valencia that after years of scheming his way up the ladder, procuring himself a position as public-works councillor, he was finally voted in for the Valencian Generalitat, to resign a month later last month, giving no plausible reason to the public, except the old ill health excuse…but if you ask me (and my Tomas will back my argument) that is a poor excuse for the rhetorical chicanery he enjoys. And nobody has since seen him. A recluse if you want my opinion. These people turn out to have many delusions in their godless lives."

"And you know where he has retired to?"

"Not really…", she tormented my heart a bit longer.

"Do you have any clue?"

"I have heard…(because even the devil has some friends…and some of them from Madrid), and they talk too loosely in the presence of simple women like me…. as I was saying…I overheard them commenting and the comment got fixed in my mind, stuck to his notorious name, that he had a house, no, an apartment in Valencia on the Avenida Del Cid, over some coffee importer from the Americas. I can't remember the country because it was so long ago."

"Thank you very much Encarna, you have been very helpful."

"Don't mention it, 'we are here to help the traveller while we keep the business going', was my mother-in-law's motto."

"Of course, how inconsiderate of me. Could I have a packet of Fortuna?" And she dropped her knitting unceremoniously and rushed to the bar-side with the grace of a gazelle. The weight of her humanity wobbled joyfully, enhancing the severity of her inherited dress.

"Light, Menthol or Normal?"

"Normal, please" I conveyed sheepishly, I had not turned to the old vice, but between potatoes, cucumbers and cigarettes, the latter were handbag friendly. She handed me a half-used matchbox as a token, in acknowledgement of my grateful gesture, always one step ahead of me.

"Is there a pay phone from where I could ring for a taxi?" I ventured just before another customer slipped in through the macaroni curtain.

"I won't hear of it. If one thing I have to say about the whole lot of them, is that their tongues are too loose for comfort. Well-paid go-betweens they are. Let me fetch my Tomas, "Tomaas!", she shouted into a side-door and from it a small man of her own age appeared like a timid rabbit from a hat, too small inside his oversized trousers of nondescript colour that hung around him by a pair of braces. It was clear who wore those trousers there by the size of them.

"You are to take the lady here wherever she needs to go Tomas", to which he acquiesced bovinely. I still remembered the Tomas of yesterday. Thomas had been twice the man he was some thirty years ago, the man who fitted in his loose trousers when they had been fashionable. There had been an extraordinary shift of bodily substance in that marriage. Mrs. Encarna had accumulated the weight he had shed; moreover, he appeared to have shed his social weight completely onto his wife to live a peaceful existence, no more pretending to be who his mother had wanted him to be. There was no longer a postmaster in that isolated establishment, because the postmistress had freed him, and he mumbled endless complaints under his breath, and nobody bothered to redress them, because we all presumed that that was his way of communicating.

"You'd better let me carry your luggage to the car, chiqueta", and there he went, moaning about the weight of the case in muffled tones. I could not let him know that my destination was the bus station to catch the last one to Valencia, to confront the retiring Councillor Antonio Benavente with his pointless lifelong threat, and to make him see the lengths I was prepared to go to unmask his sordid past if necessary. Neither could I tell him that I wanted to find my father's apartment, where my aunt went to hide my daughter. Señor Tomas was his wife's ears and eyes with his taxi services, and a very important source of informative power that fed Señora Encarna's emporium, and the town's and thereabouts. I could not risk the news of my coming to precede me; not when my daughter had recently left her grandparents' home, to look for her mother.

"She hasn't left an address but went two weeks ago to Valencia", her grandmother had confessed when I called her from England, believing me to be from the Registry Office, on my official revaluation of electoral addresses. The old woman had panicked at the mere thought of officialdom and legalities, forwarding that piece of news without reserve, in the hope of cutting short my telephone enquiries. She was protecting her granddaughter from imminent harm I instinctively felt, answering all my questions with obvious truths because she must have had the belief that a civil servant might promptly deploy nation-wide forces, in his lunch-hour, to make electoral adjustments and checks. Like most elderly people in Spain, she venerated and feared the sound of governmental titles.

She deserved my compassion in her hour of suffering, but I could not afford noble sentiments yet towards my usurper. There would be room in my heart to be magnanimous when the life of my daughter could be guaranteed…and I had seen her. Until then, I could not tell my intentions to good old serviceable Tomas; instead, I asked him to take me to my old home, in Baños.

The re-entry into my native world had been precipitated by the curiosity of my informant and rushed by the servility of her husband; though far from conscripting my freedom, the unexpected influence of others did propel me to the impetuousness that (I know now) can seldom bring regrets, as estimations of risks are what give us a false sense of danger, to end up regretting actions not taken, paths not trodden, by our own doing. It was the feeling that each step I took, being forced, fortuitous or schemed, contributed to the pattern of cogs that moved the clockwork of my fate, which gave me renewed hope. I was doing the right thing because there was no time to think.

Ed would have been proud of me.

I had found my own hope.

A beautiful free bird with transparent wings had been born of his ashes. Snippets of conversations I had had with Ed flowed within its song, very different from the old whispering breeze, elevating the prospects of a favourable outcome.

My precipitous visit to Baños had not been on my agenda, because I had not intended to overnight in Valencia, or anywhere else. My idea had been to by-pass my town and travel directly to the city; there I would negotiate with my first husband and then and not before, I would travel to Madrid to find my daughter. But I had learnt that Aurora was not in Madrid anymore, that my first husband had retired from politics, and La Señora Encarna wanted to know where I might spend my immediate time before my suspected meeting with the object of her recent cavilations. As for me, I did not wish to disclose the timing of my intentions; therefore I roamed the streets and squares until the twilight, publicly advertising to any of my former neighbours that I would be staying in town for a few days, to air the house.

The house. Home in happier years when it was grandmother's home or my aunt's after our mothers' death. It had become "the house" since I was its sole proprietor as in, the four walls and roof that belonged to me, an empty shell. My empty shell.

The inanimate shrine of my family. The only decaying

façade in the street, saved from the PVC upgrading of the recent refurbishing and prosperity.

After fifteen years of abandonment, the old oak door threw a metallic groan and cavernously surrendered its past to me. The sunken vestibule of other times resplendent cleanliness hid beneath the opaqueness of thick dust. Cobwebs hung from every corner and across the open doors and through them, the rooms oozed damp and tragedy. The atmosphere I had disturbed was rank, ungrateful. I was an intruder in my own house. A sudden drought closed the door behind me. I had to squint my eyes to make out the shadows of the upper corridor, from where noises of a struggle came...I pricked up my ears...I distinguished faint sobs and instinctively ran upstairs in the evil dark, to my old room in pursuit...of nothing that was not in my mind.

A blasphemy or two as parapet,
thrown at the void ahead of me,
did not prevent a gelid thought
of other times, to pass the spot
where sadness froze a memory.

It was not in me to wander in dark houses, to open suspicious doors and confront suspected menaces but I had to exorcise the ghosts I had created over years of fearful neglect. I was being attacked a second time, in the recess of my empty shell. The putrid scent of his unwanted presence filtered from under the only locked door in the entire house. Behind it... a quiet chaos reigned, illuminated by the faint mid-night light that the shutters could not keep out. The bedclothes and pillows were scattered where they had landed fifteen years before, during my struggle, and the bedside lamp was still on the floor, broken. I put it back in its place, and my action made a cloud of dust gather around the bed when I disturbed its dishevelled sheets. The bottom sheet, the embroidered top, a blanket, my multi coloured coverlet that grandmother had knitted for me one winter, the pillows, …I arranged them all with premeditated slowness, revisiting memories, preserving the dust accumulated between the rancid folds and wrinkles. When the last vestiges of my ordeal were straightened, I stood back to admire the new order I had mastered over my pain and revulsion, over the shame of having once wilfully bedded the man who raped me.

I looked around in the semi darkness and what I saw pleased me. There was no decay under the dust. My room, like myself, had not been corrupted. The carrion bird of hatred was his…and moribund. It had preyed on me from that unmade bed in the dark for too long. If I were to open the window, it might fly back to him…to his master.

I could hear my grandmother downstairs in the kitchen, with her usual utilitarian wisdom "No good to worry about problems you cannot solve". I had nothing left of value to my life, of which he could not deprive me of. The thought came to me that somewhere in Valencia, my daughter was looking for her mother, most probably revisiting her last days with Tita Celia.

I opened the shutters and with it my room was my own again, and that imperious urge to keep Aurora from harm came back to me afresh.

Ana and her messenger birds

I had to find him before she did.

At daybreak, I could take the last bus to Valencia, while I was still believed to be in town by all, leaving my luggage behind to keep the illusion, and I would employ the coming night on her search but...before it, I had to locate the apartment I had inherited from my missing father; the address of which, I had always have in my power unbeknown to me, among all the belongings and legal documents of my aunt, I thought.

My daughter might still remember...and I had to make sure...

I rummaged through the green leather folder that had become appendix-to-my-travels, which had once been owned by my aunt and before her by my grandmother, until the right envelope emerged. I copied the address pertaining to the deeds of a property in Valencia, put the documents back, zipped the folder without much reasoning, rushed to the kitchen and hid it inside the old stove. I wrote a few lines explaining its whereabouts and expressing my wishes over its contents, and went to mail it to Sussan and Megan in England. The Whitman sisters had been my friends and neighbours since I moved to England, and I knew they would execute the terms of my will with meticulous care, in the event of my death at the hands of retired Councillor Benavente.

Retired Councillor Antonio Benavente?

What, a man in his early forties, who has committed and sanctioned crimes, in order to grasp a glimmer of power; whom in his delirium of respectability had wronged wife and daughter so grievously, whose dream had all but materialised only a few months previously, had retired? Why? To do what? Not to serve his country from a more modest position. Not to write his infamous memoirs. It could not be to spend more time with his family. The generosity of that statement was lost in his rapacious persona. It did not ring true. There were other sinister reasons for his unnatural behaviour; the nature of which nauseated me, debilitating my resolve the more I thought of it.

Not daring to delve deeper into ideas that could frighten me, I walked to the bus station before sunset, through the streets that had seen me happier, the plaza that saw my aunt dancing during the midsummer night verbena with my father, through the mediaeval bridge that heard them parting against their will, through that passage still used as it had been through the ages, with an indentation through the middle of its path turning rivulet on wet days. A memory of my father had been imprinted in my heart, indelibly linked to that bridge, with its parapets worn out where elbows had rested through the centuries to admire the scenery or say goodbye to loved ones.

I had come from a man as well as my two mothers, one that had loved me and had loved my aunt to his destruction. A good man deserving of my aunt's forgiveness and mine.

18 THE WRONG ADDRESS

At that early hour, the bus to Valencia travelled very light due to the nature of the business that took the mostly female day-trippers to the provincial capital, like specialists, legalities, or shopping for clothes and unnecessary products.

The journey gave me an hour in which to ponder on the favourable change of my native town because there had taken place an architectural refurbishment during the years of my absence, where the squalor of the regime had been eradicated with pride in the detail. Important public facades had been renovated, the fountains were cleaned, street-lighting was completed, public gardens were lovingly tended, PVC windows installed everywhere, and also the general demeanour of my once oppressed neighbours was relaxed, at peace with each other.

People walked noisily to and from the shops and homes. The younger generation ambled aimlessly, entertained with each other's company and pocket-sized personal stereos. The older ones born under the old regime had lost their austerity, being even affable to old enemies. Democracy walked amiably on that perfect May morning I left behind, on my way to Valencia. In the various villages and towns, we drove through to pick up the odd passenger. There were signs of a tightly fought general and council election. Dotted around street corners, stuck to shop windows, and hanging from street lamps like mediaeval standards, the political slogans and written pledges screamed aloud for the attention of the voters, well ahead of the local elections. There seemed to be a dozen or so political parties competing for their proportional representation in the local councils. Though it was a foregone conclusion that my town had, and will always, vote for the left; a habit not lost after three decades and a half of dictatorship.

I was still indulging in the virtues of social and political freedom twenty years on, at the back of the bus, when it stopped with a jerk at the untimely request of someone by the roadside. I had not noticed the route we had taken but it was the national N3 where my mother and grandmother died twenty years ago, and that stop was the same spot where the bomb went off. An old woman got on while another very tall one alighted unnoticed by all that had not known her. She was my mother and that roadside adorned with fresh chrysanthemums was her final stop. My mother had found her resting-place in her private universe, unhindered by the tortuous illness that destroyed her former existence, amidst the bunches of flowers and coloured ribbons adorning a simple cross planted there, by the roadside where it all happened two decades ago. It had become a bus stop nowadays, perhaps by popular demand in a stand against terrorism, perhaps because the relatives of the victims needed a shrine where to place their anguish.

It was my mother's final stop, and she left the bus and my life without a last glance, hardly noticing me as she had done when alive. I scanned the bus checking all my fellow travellers until I saw my last Guardian angel.

My Aunt Celia remained seated in the front of the bus, where she had been travelling, by her sister. Of all, she had been the most talkative ghost, the most persistent as she had been in life, the last of my relatives she was in death the most loyal of my dead. From then onwards, my mission took a double significance: I had to give my Aunt the peace she had died for, the peace of finding my daughter, for her sake, for Aurora herself, for my own peace.

We arrived at the bus terminal and left it on foot, in the direction of the historical centre, to loiter until the evening, and then begin combing the central arteries of the city, but I had not foreseen the limitations of my memories. Events and places had stood still while Valencia had adapted to modernity. The old diverted river I remembered as the dried-up chasm dividing the city on its way to the Mediterranean, half wasteland, and half unauthorised playground, had been transformed. In its place meandered a sinuous green belt. A series of parks, small open-air theatres, manicured walkways, and sport's fields ran through it, making it a pleasure to cross the innumerable bridges that took me to the centre. In the late evening hour when the nocturnal life of the town started, the city workers were already heading for the long bars in the cafes. They ambled in small groups on their way to the Ruzafa district to sample some tapas before dinner at home, and there were groups of mature women of my own age, strolling three abreast at a time, chatting about their lives while they glanced here and there to find the best outdoor table where to smoke. Couples ambled in zigzag avoiding contact with the human tide roaming the pavements. Here and there people strove to find a seat in the Valencian night, in the outside tables to smoke at large, as if it were the first or the last time. It was too crowded to accomplish my mission. I knew it was a long walk to my father's home but who of you would have accelerated a chance encounter with retired Councillor Benavente?

I needed the cover of darkness. I took to crossing the main bridges leading to the El Carmen Quarter, walking on the North and South of the river until well past the Valencian dinner time, and then, I found the appropriate spot through the San José bridge. I merged with the evening tide, always preceded by my Aunt and protected by the yellowing street lighting of the old quarters on my way to the square Plaza de la Reina, from where I intended to reach the back streets of the Town Hall. Tita Celia appeared and vanished in hallucinatory flashes; at one time her image and mine were reflected on the same display window, between summer mannequins both of us of similar age, both looking alike.

Did my daughter Aurora look like us?

Would I recognise her in the multitude of faces of the night?

I left the culture and leisure area for the alleyways of the historic centre, heading for the professional district around the two squares, bastion of doctors, lawyers and landladies in competition for space with the anachronistic and narrow turn of the century shops and bullied by heavier civil service departments. Except for the hostels and some hotels, every establishment was closed and soon only my Aunt and I were roaming the silent streets of the old centre. A palpitating silence descended through the rooftops of eighteen and nineteen century buildings onto doorways and basement windows. There was another set of footsteps reverberating on the narrow pavements, when I knew perfectly well that my aunt was immaterial, hence unable to produce stepping sounds. Someone was walking with us. Someone who stopped when I did so. I tried calling my Aunt for reinforcements and the echo of my voice tried too, behind me in the dark. I quickened my pace inspecting every street placard until the right address was divined more than read at the entrance to a side street off the Calle Colón, named "Carrer de la Veritat". It was number sixteen I wanted, in a stretch of no more than thirty yards. Surely the address could not be right. I scanned the empty street against the luminosity of the perpendicular avenue at the other end, unable to see my Aunt in the silhouetted shapes between that brightness and me. My Aunt was not there. The second set of footsteps was approaching from behind. I ran into that narrow street for want of common sense. In other times when I was more thoughtful and less inclined to die for unnatural causes, I might have frozen between the thoughts of entering a possible trap or facing my pursuer but that night however, the light of that interjecting avenue was stronger than my character. On either side of the alleyway, there were only commercial backstreet exits. I ran to the light at the end of it, to an avenue of royal proportions, and turned to the left where another placard mentioned its name, and at that, I felt my blood crystallising in my veins. A cold dread weakened my most determined intentions at the sight of that old coffee shop of undefined coloured panelling and shabby awning. It traded under the name of "Café de Colombia, de Exportación". By its side, a residential entrance of Art Deco design was crowned with the number sixteen and above it hung a set of four floors of elegant balconies, spread in sensuous curves and railing-work covered in city grime. That must be the retreat of retired Councillor Benavente…and my father's house…, both in the same building. The door was ajar.

My aunt had a habit of not closing doors behind herself.

Those steps were audible again from the side-street I had just left but this time it was deliberation on my part, to slip through the inviting door and close it behind me, so I would know for sure whether my pursuer had a key to it or he was just lost in the maze of alleyways.

I waited five minutes in the shadows, and nothing happened. The threatening footsteps had merged with the rest of the noises of the avenue and the door remained safely closed. My blood turned back to its original liquid state; not that I was not aware of my still delicate position, but two sources of danger were confusing even to the most rational nature. But it was an advantage to know who my enemy inside the building was, for which I was eternally grateful to the Postmistress Encarna.

I made myself familiar with my surroundings guided by the streetlight filtered through the leaded-glass design above the front door. It sent a dark impression of a lotus flower across the hall. There I noticed the elaborate ironwork of the elevator's double-doors and its cage. The black and white tiles on the floor and the ornate vine balustrade of the staircase were still the original features of that type of building, so common in the Valencia of the thirties.

I went up the stairs in semidarkness, very quietly spying the noises within the building, with my left hand gripping the kitchen knife inside my handbag, and once on the first floor, I switched the light on to read the door-names but neither my father or my ex-husband's name owned the two doors on that flight of stairs. I climbed the second flight passing another lotus window and read again and again on the third floor. There I stopped after that third reading proved fruitless and sat on the steps beneath the landing, to consume the last seconds of light, certain by then that I had no more choices left, no more stairs, no more delay in giving a shape and substance to my furtive ideas. There were not two apartments on the fourth floor, one of my father's and one of Councillor Tony's because attics in this period building only had one domiciled door, as the second was always for access to the roof terrace.

Abominable thoughts began to take shape.

When Antonio abducted my daughter from my father's home, where my aunt was hiding her, he already knew the address from the days of terror and surveillance of suspected sympathisers. And he must have known of its perennial vacancy, since my aunt had died, and he had forced me out of the country, and probably believed me ignorant of my inheritance from the father I had never met. It must have been an attractive refuge from where to conduct his dubious machinations. If I had known then…I might have never…and even now, I was not to know of his recent machinations, as we never notice the multiple paths of others running along ours, that cross our lives.

We can only walk over the path we see.

It was around ten o'clock in the evening, for which it was highly probable to be his dinnertime. He would be indoors or about to come home. To come home to the house of my father, the house from where my daughter was taken, my house. My sense of justice was revolting against his usurpation. His ambition had cast a long shadow over my entire life, while he trampled over my father's grave, assuming his property. The man had blighted my family, and was enjoying the spoils. The indoctrination I received as a child at the hands of my mother, in her lucid years, foretold eternal damnation for lesser crimes than those hidden in his suitcase, and for a while it seemed an appropriate punishment.

Twenty years on, the national past buried for good, without imparting justice, only left the belief on divine retribution, but I didn't have faith. Moreover, matters of conscience, required to have one, with which to be punished with.

Doubting the existence of the retired Councillor's

conscience, it was painful to see him prosper in this world, and to visualise the peace of his hereafter days. To my own chagrin, there I was, on the landing, prepared to sign a truce or to die, whichever happened first, to keep my daughter from harm.

More thoughts began to take shape…

I was armed, I could defend myself if necessary…but would I find the peace I was looking for?

I was in the dark at the mercy of the third lotus window and my sense of hearing had sharpened by the proximity of danger. A doorbell rang on the fourth floor. A feminine mature voice audible through the closed door answered through the intercom and a hideous buzz foreign in that architecture opened the entrance door three floors below. The newcomer switched the landing lights on again, opened the double set of doors of the elevator with as many groans as did the old metallic hinges, climbed on it huffing and puffing and began the ascent. The rudimentary system of cogs and pulleys that animated the lift did resent the weight of the climber; making its disapproval felt by a series of screeching laments, like those of the tormented ghost made to drag his chains for eternity. It was an awfully slow process of starts and stops and small adjustments that took longer than the egg-timing of the landing lights. The elevator conquered the third floor vaguely illuminated by the streetlamps from beyond the lotus window, and it produced pockets of pitch-black density outside its range of vision, where I hid. There were two riders in the ageing contraption. The persons in the elevator were discernible by contrasts.

Ana and her messenger birds

The man occupied most of the room inside, commending himself to God every time the lift hiccupped. His anatomy consisted of pneumatic material stuffed with generous dinners and communion-wine, badly contained under his black clothes. He wore his dog collar with mal-repressed arrogance. Councillor Benavente's alliances had not changed much.

The other passenger was my Aunt Celia.

I followed their ascent in the dark, sliding through the walls of the staircase until it was not safe to continue. On the fourth floor my Aunt stretched one hand out and wrapped it around the inter-locking bars of the first set of doors, preventing their opening while the Priest fumbled with both locks for some time, cursing the 'damned old thing'. Aunt Celia released her hold just before panic set in the robust features of the holy man, saw him out of his cage and slowly turned into thin air. She had not seen me or appeared no to, so intent she had been on playing her trick. She had looked charming and excited during her exploits, as in the days of my childhood playing hide and seek.

I tiptoed my way back to the steps below the third landing, to spy the sounds again, from the safety of the two lawyers' offices. Upstairs, the same mature voice ushered the released priest indoors, in muffled tones all very hush-hush. Downstairs someone closed the front door and made for the stairs in the dark. I recognised the footsteps of my earlier pursuer on the first floor, though the resonance was sharper on the landing. I retreated to door number six, careful not to brush against any of the switches of that corner, holding my breath and counting the climbing steps of my pursuer. I went over my mental list of duties for the last time. I had spent the past two weeks tidying my legal affairs, and those of poor Ed and travelling, battling with my apprehensions, thinking, putting my dead relatives to rest…and I had come to terms with my unlived life; therefore in the event of my early death, every detail had been taken care of, and the time had come to conquer one last fear, if only that nagging pain in my heart would clear, that yearning to see my daughter, to know that she was happy…to explain to her so that she might not think ill of me.

So much longing for so very few memories to take with me.

A shadow walked across the third lotus window below. My pursuer was not foreign to my surroundings, having no need for door names or light. I tried to conjure up my Aunt Celia to no avail. As my last resort, I opened my handbag, took out the knife and hid my armed hand behind my back in readiness, startling my interloper with that motion as the blade shone under the moonlight. My pursuer, having as I stepped onto the third landing accustomed to the same darkness, did not have time to see my weapon, only its reflection.

It was a woman. A very young Aunt Celia.

She recoiled to the number five door opposite in surprise. We measured each other, calculating risks for a few seconds and gradually relaxed our guard. She looked at me trying to recognise me, for a time that seemed endless, in which I also perceived her features, which were as familiar to me, as those of my aunt, although she had short hair, and was not dressed as I remembered her.

"Are you my Aunt Celia?" She asked in a whisper. The knife slipped from my hand, and fell to the floor, with a thud that only the two of us noticed.

It was my daughter, who had confused me in the darkness.

My daughter, who I had not instinctively recognized.

My daughter, whom my maternal instinct now claimed as mine, was in front of me, after so many years, and I did not know what to do, or what to say, or how to correct her mistake, without breaking the bond that had kept her as part of my life as the girl she had been last time I saw her. My daughter, now a woman, blurred the image that I had kept in my memory.

"Aunt Celia?" She repeated in a very low voice, as if the night knew our secrets, and as if we both knew that it was imperative to keep our presence hidden. The fourth-floor apartment seemed to gravitate over our consciousness.

"I am your mother, Aurora" I confessed, afraid of breaking the spell of the past; afraid to face the romantic or hateful idea that in my absence, she might have created of me.

"Mom…?" She said slowly, listening to the meaning of the word, which she hadn't used for so long. "But, they did tell me that you were sick, dying, and that my aunt couldn't take care of me alone, and that it was better that way. Are you sure you're not dead, like Aunt Celia?"

"I am alive, Aurora. I spoke to your grandmother on the phone, and she told me where I could find you."

"Oh, Mom, you've been dead for so long", she lamented without reproach, without asking why I hadn't come to see her, but neither of us moved in our positions, paralyzed by the enormity of emotions that filled the space between us.

"Your grandparents would have told you for your own good."

"No, not them; It wasn't them. It was my father who told them. They only believed their son, and I believed them, you know, because I was a girl, and I trusted those who loved me, because they have been good to me, and because Aunt Celia didn't come back for me, and I was alone, and I only had them, and you didn't come to pick me up."

My daughter tried to defend her grandparents, and although it hurt me, I knew that it was natural for her to love them, like the parents they had been to her.

"Tita Celia died that night with a broken heart, for not having been able to protect you, and I had to leave you in their care to protect you."

We stood there swimming in a heavy sea of revelations with the landing between us, unsure of what to feel, what to do, what to say to bridge the abyss that separated our lives. My daughter and I. Aurora and I at last.

"I died too, mother. Nobody has called me daughter since then."

"No-one has called me mother since you were taken from me."

"Please mom, say my name again", Aurora implored in the distance.

We were exchanging five years of memories, and fifteen of our life experience in whispers, adhered to each other's doors number five and number six, unable to see what we looked like. Later on, life might happen to us, what lay behind the door on the fourth floor might separate us or let us be one, who could say? Meanwhile we were delaying taking any action, at a loss in our new reality.

"Aurora", new dawn, I whispered. "Aurora suits you" I said, coming out of my cavilations, not finding beautiful things to tell her, after raking our past for shared anecdotes or memories connecting the young woman opposite me, with the girl and the mother we had once been. I had not foreseen my inability to articulate a lifetime of missing her. I could not voice my fifteen years of longing without breaking down. There was a chaos of words impossible to string together in a coherent sense to fit the situation we were in. My shaking knees could not hold me against the door.

"Do you mind if I sit down, Aurora?" We sat close to each other in the same second step going up to the Attic floor and remained there quietly and self-contained. Our respective tragedies were not exchangeable material on that first encounter and the love we once shared had been left behind our own present lives. Other kinds of love had blossomed in the emptiness left.

The blade of the unused knife sparkled on the welcome mat of the Number Six door, calling for attention.

"Are you in trouble, mom?"

"We both are," I said remembering the business that had brought me there.

"Who lives upstairs?"

"My first husband…your father"

"My father?" she mused. "Then it's true that Tita Celia gave me to my father…"

"Oh, no! She brought you here to my father's house to keep you from harm, but your father found you, because he knew where to look. I did not expect to meet your father upstairs squatting in my father's apartment. I came to this address making time, delaying the encounter between him and I, with the hope of finding you here before he did, because your grandmother to me you were travelling in this direction. There are two addresses to the same building, or there must have been a trader's entrance through the side-street when my father was alive."

"Is he dead?" she was wondering, meaning to ask instead, "are you completely alone?"

"The old regime killed him", I abridged the truth. "I never met him. Are you close to yours?" There was reluctance in the air around my daughter, but she eventually opened up.

"I was only recently told who he was, and all I know is that he is the man who told me that you were dying, fifteen years ago in the flat above us now, but I don't wish him ill, not now", she repeated with deliberation as she reached for my hand and pressed. "Not now."

At that, the door above us opened and the landing light followed it on. I reached for the knife indicating with my index to maintain complete silence. A social farewell was taking place upstairs. The mature feminine voice of earlier could not hold her calm for long between sighs and references to God. Her interlocutor sounded impatient. "Come, come Vicenta. It's not good, nor godly to wish him alive still in his condition, as you know as a nurse. God has been merciful in his designs."

"But only forty-one years…at the peak of his life, when he had it all…"

"Cancer makes no distinction between those who have it all and those who have nothing. It's God who does the choosing my good woman, and Him alone must have a reason for it."

The priest opened the elevator's door unnecessarily, because the said Vicenta did not let the priest go. "I don't dispute you father, but to rush it, so that not even you were at his side to give him the absolution he had been crying for."

"If it had not been for that wretched door…that's why we can't postpone our peace with our Lord, as I keep stressing to my flock, though the Confessional is seldom used nowadays, Vicenta, and there might not be a priest close at hand when our time comes."

"I sure did call you as soon as he requested it, Father."

"Don't trouble yourself, Vicenta, you have been a great help to Don Antonio. If any blame has to be apportioned, it would fall on these rusted lift doors that seemed to have a will of their own and they have prevented me from carrying out my duties; let's hope he had no grave sins to be absolved from."

A noisy blow of a handkerchief and a rosary of sniffs from the woman urged the priest to open the lift doors saying, "Compose yourself, woman. There a wake to prepare. Didn't he have a daughter?"

"Now that you say it; he did try to contact some relatives but there had been no reply forthcoming of his liking."

"As I said, it's a pity to postpone matters of conscience",

and the lift began its painful descent bearing its onerous cargo and the repeated farewell of the woman plummeted after it, half finished, half-heard and half-wanted. The landing lights went off again, securing our anonymity in the building, while Vicenta retired indoors to prepare the wake. The lift passed us in the dark, threatening to drop its load at any time; which sent the holy man into a frenzy of activity, and loud imprecations unbecoming of his collar, until he was safely out of it four floors below us, when the lights were switched on again before the street door closed behind him.

My daughter and I saw each other for the first time in detail, recognising who we had been before we were divided. We looked so much like Tita Celia when she was our respective ages. We were portraits of that same sitter, in two stages of completion.

"Tita Celia rests in peace now, Aurora", I thought aloud. And I thought of my dead, who somehow, their lives and deaths, their dreams and horrors, were inextricably linked to the city, as if Valencia was a mythical bird, an utopian place that sadly, they never conquered, because life got in their way. With Antonio dead, that Valencia would be mine, mine and my daughter's.

"Do you want to see your father for the last time?", I asked her, dreading the answer.

My daughter took my hand to her lap as she said, still speaking in whispers: "No, I don't want to, I don't need to, not anymore. ¿Would you like to tell me what happened in detail?"

"I have a long story to tell you, and a unique garden to

show you in England. Would you like to travel with me that far?, Aurora"

"You still have to show me Valencia, as you once promised me, remember?"

"We'll do it tomorrow. First we have to find somewhere to spend the night."

We also have to go to our village.

And I had an envelope to open as well.

The last farewell from Ed.

Now I could do so.

The end

ABOUT THE AUTHOR

This is my first novel, which I have written over a long period of time, alternating my writing with my teaching.

I was born in Spain during Franco's dictatorship, and came to England in the mid-eighties, where I settled, and began teaching. I have always written poetry, always wanted to write fiction, and always wanted to be a teacher. The time has come for me to write. The mission I set for myself many years ago was to present the forgotten and overlooked stories of women, and their perspective of national and personal events, often obscured as part of a male narrative.

Printed in Great Britain
by Amazon

42560515R00136